Splitting Heirs

Michael Franklin

PublishAmerica
Baltimore

© 2005 by Michael Franklin.
All rights reserved. No part of this book may be reproduced, stored in a retrieval system or transmitted in any form or by any means without the prior written permission of the publishers, except by a reviewer who may quote brief passages in a review to be printed in a newspaper, magazine or journal.

First printing

At the specific preference of the author, PublishAmerica allowed this work to remain exactly as the author intended, verbatim, without editorial input.

ISBN: 1-4137-8044-X
PUBLISHED BY PUBLISHAMERICA, LLLP
www.publishamerica.com
Baltimore

Printed in the United States of America

1

1938

Kurt Feldman stood at the large window of his first floor library and looked out towards the Aller. The river itself — nearly a mile away — was invisible across the flatlands, but distant buildings on its bank marked its line. It had stopped raining at last, but myriad drops of water still clung to the glass, adding further obscurity to the late November misty afternoon.

He was waiting for his grandson to appear — as he had been for the last two days. He knew that the lad would be facing difficulties. He shrugged his shoulders and turned back towards the large table in the center of the room. Things had to be said. The time had come. He moved across to put another log of wood on the open fire. The glowing redness awoke to fresh flame, and flickering light reflected on the somber paneling, illuminating the ranks of books and highlighting the colors of their bindings. The fresh crackling was the only audible sound. A fragrance rose from the burning pine.

Yes — times were changing, he knew only too well and painfully. The euphoria that had emerged to support the Fuhrer had gladdened the hearts of millions of Germans, and he acknowledged that there was a sense of destiny and national unity emerging now in 1938 that contrasted well with the disasters of the Weimar Republic years following the last war. He knew that he was part of a minority who saw clearly beyond the short-term merits of noisy national accord, recognizing that this unfettered dictatorship was fostering a cult of cruelty in preference to one of natural justice. Greater Germany had caved in to the demands of the Nazis for power. Old Hindenburg — the failing president — had submitted. The *Sudetenland* was being claimed, an annexing that arrogantly ignored international disapproval. Now the *Anschluss*. Austria had been absorbed. It would get worse before it got better.

Kurt had another compelling reason for caution. He was a Jew. His race in Germany had already heard the knell of doom very clearly. For several years now they had felt the disapproval of the wider population — public insults, businesses picketed, windows broken, forced removal, children threatened, humiliation. That unjust distaste was now — with the encouragement of the new ruler — amplifying into hatred and cruelty. Where would it end?

A book lay open on the table. He had been reading it intermittently — Goethe. The finely balanced prose had once brought him joy. Now it generated frustration. With higher thought vanishing from real life, it was difficult to relish it between the pages of a book. He closed it reverently, but deliberately, and returned to sit in the big red leather chair by the fire, gazing into its depths. He dozed.

It was darkening when the crunch of wheels on his gravel drive roused him. He went down the wide stairs to the large hall, crossing the wooden floor to the front porch. He opened the door, stepping back as he did so. His grandson, immaculate in *Luftwaffe* uniform, cap in hand, came briskly in. His smile was genuine, but he instantly took the door from his grandfather and closed it. It was clear that he did not want to be seen in this place. The old man acquiesced. He understood. It was as he expected. They shook hands warmly. The younger man asked: "Is there anyone else here?"

"No Gunther. I knew it would be prudent to be on my own. Come on up."

Grandfather led the way back to the library, his guest restraining his more sprightly abilities to allow his elderly host to make the ascent at a measured pace. In the library they faced each other. Gunther, aware of the welcoming warmth of the open fire, but with apparent reluctance, undid his leather belt, and removed his long grey uniform coat to reveal his tunic, the wings of a pilot, and the bars of an *Oberleutnant*. He said: "Your note did not give me much choice. I risk much in coming to see you, but apparently I risk much by not coming — according to you."

Kurt, for the moment, did not answer. He moved to the fire, took a spill from a jar on the mantelpiece, lit it, and transferred the flame to an oil lamp on the table, replacing the glass carefully. He had, it was true, written to his grandson demanding a meeting — a letter expressed in language that brooked no refusal. They had not met for three years.

Kurt's descendants had deliberately contrived to separate themselves from Jewishness. He himself had married a gentile, Inge Muller, whom he had loved dearly, and she him. Their son Johann, who had distinguished himself in the First World War, had taken the name Muller and had also married a gentile. Thus Gunther, though a quarter Jewish, appeared not to be. The increasing dilution of each generation away from its origins was now seen as fortunate. It had enabled Johann and Gunther to live and prosper as perceived pure Germans, and they had been careful to construct their lives to achieve this apparent conformity.

The racial divergence had not meant that Kurt's son and grandson had ceased to feel deep affection for him. And they had loved the now deceased Inge. As grandfather and grandson stood in the flickering firelight there was — each knew, and each felt — love between them. Gunther's education and the social status his father and mother had achieved, may have opened his door of opportunity wide, and he was now part of the new Germany, but childhood memories of the kindness of this now aged man could not be forgotten.

Kurt asked: "A brandy — something to eat?"

Gunther shook his head.

"Where are you staying?"

"Celle. I found a room at the *Stadlerhoff.*"

"I wrote to you at home, but where did you have to come from?"

"Dusseldorf."

Grandfather gestured at the uniform. His emotions were a mixture of distaste and pride. The pride showed. "You appear to be doing well. Your father is pleased?"

"Certainly."

It had been two full years since Kurt had seen his son. "How are things with him, and your mother?"

"Good. Father is back in uniform again often these days. His involvement in the civil and business affairs in Munich has earned him much respect over time, and he has some responsibilities now. His Major's rank at the end of the last war has been restored to him, and he is leading a *Volksturm* unit."

"That pleases him?"

Gunther shrugged. "Grandfather — it is not really a question of whether it pleases him or not. It has become a duty. I can understand that you will feel distant from what is happening in our country, but for most of us now there is a mission. We have been through bad times and we now have glorious opportunity to show the rest of the world that we will not be sat upon. Of course Father sees that — as does Mother, and everyone I know. If we all act together now under the leadership of the *Fuhrer*, then better times will come."

"But not for me, or for many thousands like me — we are being blown aside."

"The plain fact is that the Jewish people prospered more than most during the recession period, so it must not surprise them now that they are being asked to pay the price."

"That — my boy — may be popular sentiment now, but, in your case, it ignores the fact that I funded your father's business and gave it frequent financial help in the early days, and bought as a gift the family home in which you were brought up. And what do you consider a fair price for we Jews to pay — the forceful dispossession of our homes and businesses? The undeserved taint of dishonor? Do you think that our neighboring nations are going to be full of admiration for this attitude?"

"Our neighboring nations have hardly been generous to us since the war. The Treaty of Versailles was a disgrace. The French and English are going to have to mind their manners now, and they will certainly have to respect us. Herr Hitler talks gloriously of a fight for *Lebensraum,* expanding our borders to the east. For twenty years they have laughed at us in France, England, America, and elsewhere, but things will change now. The communists have been crushed here, and they will be forced to abandon the idiocy of their philosophy elsewhere. The *Duce* in Italy has paved the way. He will support us. The good times will return. You used to talk to me of the glory of the Hapsburgs, and the greatness of Germany when you were young. Well — Grandfather — it should not surprise you that most of us are joyful that we may see greatness here again."

The young man's voice had risen as he had spoken, but he was suddenly aware that he was talking offensively to a cherished relative. He dropped his head, became silent, and turned to face the fire.

The old man moved quietly across and sat in his fireside chair. Another faced him, but Gunther declined to claim it. He walked back towards the window, reaching out to draw the heavy curtains across. Then he turned to his grandfather again. "I should tell you that we do worry about you. Of course we are aware of the financial support that you have given and we are grateful for it. We are not happy that we have to keep our distance. My father wanted me to tell you that. We just do not know how we can change things." He shrugged his shoulders again. "Was it because you have not seen so much of us that you asked me to come here? Your letter mentioned a last act that you had to perform, but none of us that know you would presume that meant you were going to take your own life."

His grandfather remained silent. Gunther wandered the shelves, running a hand across the books at shoulder level, caressing the old leather bindings. He turned again to face the fire. "You appear to have remained free of the persecutions. Can you continue to do so?"

Kurt lay back in his chair. He lifted his head to look directly at his grandson. "Gunther — I am leaving Germany. My plans are made. I have no intention of staying to suffer the same fate as the Jews are undergoing now. And I am sure that I cannot expect any help from your father. I have things to tell you — important things. One of my consolations at this moment is that it is apparent you remain fond of me. Had I supposed it may be otherwise my attitude would be somewhat different. I could not know how you felt until you got here, but I am consoled that warmth remains."

"Why did you ask me to come, rather than Father? We were puzzled about that."

"Because you will benefit from certain arrangements I have made, and so will your two small daughters, whom I have never seen incidentally. Your father, still my cherished son, is now in middle age, and he may be too old when the time comes."

"When what time comes?"

"I am coming to all that Gunther. Be a little patient. I cannot rush my explanations, and it is important that you understand them fully. It is possible that we shall meet again — but unlikely." Kurt rose, reached for a cigar box on the mantelpiece, opened it, and offered it to his grandson. Gunther took one, reached for a spill, and they were silent for several moments, savoring the Cuban quality.

Resignedly, Gunther took the other fireside chair. He had hoped to be in and out quickly, but now realized that it would be a longer encounter than he had hoped, and being here with his grandfather — still beloved — brought feelings of reconciliation and revived happy memories. At least he was consoled that he had prepared carefully for this visit, covering his tracks at each stage, and ensuring that he was not followed. This was an isolated spot. He was on legitimate leave from his base. No one would know. His attitude to the Jews of Germany was now typical of the common disaffection, but he knew that they could not all be tarred with the same brush. It offended him, for instance, that the music of Mendelsohn should now be forbidden public performance.

Kurt leant forward, bringing his face closer to his grandson's. "This meeting concerns my wealth. I have been, and remain, a rich man. You will be partly aware of that. You will know that your grandmother and I lived in comfort on our estate near Hamburg. You spent many of your holidays there, roaming the spaces and enjoying all the facilities, including my yacht. You also know, as I have just mentioned, that it was my money that set your father up in Munich in 1919. It had paid for his education and it was to pay for yours. Yes — I bought his first house there, before you were born, and set him up in the business that still prospers despite the depressions down the years. Let's face it, hoteliers do better than most, particularly in a beautiful region like Bavaria. People will travel and they must eat when they do. I have always been glad that he had a good business head on him, and has made the best of his opportunities. My early help was not wasted."

He went on, speaking slowly. "What you will not be aware of is the extent and complexity of my financial affairs over the years. My father left me a small but well-run meat business in Hamburg — two slaughterhouses and a chain of eleven retail shops. Jewish or not, I had the advantage of a good education at a time when we could command it along with everyone else. I was single-minded in my ambition to succeed, particularly after your grandmother — whom I loved dearly — had agreed to marry me, and brought some wealth of her own into our partnership. That was in 1892. Hamburg was prospering and money made money. By 1897 I had diversified and was the port's third largest shipbuilder, and, in parallel, had bought several farms so that I could integrate the meat business from production to sale. I chose my managers carefully, motivated them thoroughly, and paid them well."

He paused to draw on his cigar, waving a hand through the rich smoke to disperse it. "I built a six-thousand ton ship for a firm in Bremerhavn. Well — shortly before its launching they had some financial troubles. I was hard headed then and demanded their remaining assets to pay for the ship. Thus I found myself in the shipping business, running from Hamburg and Kiel to North America. This was highly profitable done properly, and by 1902 I had two companies — one public, in which I had a majority holding, and the other private. Together, the two companies operated fourteen cargo ships, working worldwide. Refrigeration had just become practical in ships, so I was among the very first to bring meat from South America. This enabled me to increase the profitability of my retail chain across north Germany dramatically, buying out failing competitors. I also branched out into property as funds and profits began to surplus well — just land and buildings in small and large lots, leased out to whoever wanted them and could pay."

Gunther was spellbound, listening intently. His grandfather went on. " When it was apparent that the *Kaiser* was going to throw his weight about with the French and his relatives in Britain, Germany was jubilant, as it is now. This was a prosperous and confident nation. But I was worried even then — not about the as yet unseen attitude to us Jews, but realistically I simply could not see us winning a war, and I acted accordingly to protect my increasing wealth. For instance, I thought that my ships would be an essential part of national supply in wartime, but I also believed that they could be sunk if the going got hard, or confined to harbor, thus becoming a loss. So I sold them to companies that were infected by the euphoria at the time — Germany is unbeatable and all that. This process liberated funds, but I did not channel them into German business. Instead it seemed prudent, and I have proved the point, to spread the money abroad, using the Swiss banking system as a transit, to invest in places as far away and South Africa and America."

"The war came and went of course, and your grandmother and I survived it better than most. People still wanted meat. Our main anxiety was the welfare of your father — always in the thick of the fighting it seemed. We were joyful that he survived. After the war I was able to buy a lot of property, the resale of which has kept the coffers full in the post-war years, depressions or not."

"So far so good, but around 1930 I had fresh worries — the emergence of national socialism, and its bloody confrontations with the reds. I could not know where this would lead, and I was not sure that I could protect my own mobility, traveling as I wished, and buying and selling as I saw fit. As a race we were already beginning to feel the pressure. So I sold most of my residual German investments, including all my private and commercial properties, with the exception of this estate and the meat business. So I was now very cash rich. I had to consider what to do with it. If there was to be a European tumult, would Switzerland remain free of it? Probably not.

Would it be safe for me in German banks? Certainly not. The answer — right or wrong — seemed to lie overseas — put the money into land and property in stable places that would accept foreign investment. You will remember that your grandmother died at that time — a tragic event for me, but at least I now only had to think in terms of my own movements and destiny."

"In 1933 I made a lot of journeys, assessing the stability and suitability of several countries as targets for my money. I made contact with Jewish communities in a number of places, re-opening connections with many people whose close ancestors had moved from Germany to seek better times when I was small. Thus I was able to identify, with local and dependable advice, many opportunities for safe investment."

"One of the countries I went to was Canada, and that became the focus for the relocation of my wealth. There is a strong and thriving Jewish community in Quebec. My knowledge of the French language helped."

"Why pick on Canada, you may ask? Well — the reason is that I expect it to remain politically and socially stable for the next seventeen years. Why seventeen years? Because I have set things up in such a way that it will not be until 1955 that you and your children can claim my estate. The reason for the wait until 1955 is that I expect Germany, and, indeed, probably the whole of Europe, to be in turmoil before long. The saber rattling is now well underway. I hope and believe that Europe will have returned to stability by the mid-fifties. By that time you will be in middle age, and your daughters will be grown up, but you will all benefit. Your father will be elderly, but he has done well anyway and I am less concerned about rewarding him."

"I happen to believe that Britain is unbeatable, not necessarily because her resources and will are sufficient now to meet a threat from Germany, but because I know that America will come in on her side, as will all her dominions, including Canada, Australia and New Zealand, and the rest. We know from the last war how determined Britain can be when pressed. The Belgians shrug their shoulders, the French are better at talking than fighting, and the Italians have to have a sleep in the afternoon — war or not — but the British are formidable and honorable, and we would be wise to remember that. It has always been obvious to me that their qualities of honesty and endurance were passed on with the migrants to their dominions, including America originally."

Gunther looked at this grandfather in astonishment. "Could you not simply have given all this money to us now? Why the elaborate planning? Canada? It's madness — surely...." He tailed off, affronted and puzzled. "Why did you not just leave the money in a Swiss bank? We could have gone to find it when European politics become stable again under our leadership"

His grandfather shook his head. "Yes — it's madness, but what are the alternatives? You and I have different visions at this moment. Yours is of a mighty Germany that will overcome all resistance if it should come to an armed confrontation with France or whatever, surviving to become the richest and most powerful nation in Europe, offering a happy and settled place to all its citizens. My vision, and that is the one that has to count for me — is of a Germany that has responded unrealistically to the brazen leadership of a madman, who will not be able to survive the combined weight of arms that must eventually confront him."

"Certainly our nation has been depressed. Certainly the Treaty of Versailles was unjust and over-restrictive. Certainly there should be a promise of better times, but your way is not the way it should be done. Answering your question — yes, investment in Canada is a bizarre destiny for German wealth, but it is safe, and the money is there for you or the girls to claim once the inevitable furies have subsided. I know I can depend on my acquisitions to hold their value, and any other means of passing a prosperous future on to you would be fraught with risk."

Gunther leaned forward, pointing his smoldering cigar, held between finger and thumb, at his grandfather. "It is utter stupidity. All those years wasted. How will you know that the investments can be recovered to us? Have you assured yourself that they are safe from intervention of some sort — government acts that confiscate foreign owned assets — things like that. So much can change in that time."

Kurt shook his head slowly. "There are some certainties in this life, and I am sure of this one. I have friends there. You may not respect and admire my status, but they do. The costs will be met. There is a dedication to God involved. These are honest people. We share a culture and a faith. You may depend on it – it will be there when you want it."

"Has it occurred to you that the *Wehrmacht* could be running Quebec in 1955? What then for the Jews — trusted or not?"

Kurt shook his head gravely. "Take it from me young man. The great emerging German influence will not be allowed to go that far. If you want to ask yourself a more serious question, it would be what chance have I, a military aviator, got of surviving to see the day, and — an equally sad prospect — are my wife and daughter going to survive to be there?"

They both fell silent for a moment, looking into the redness of the fire. Gunther said: "Well — I cannot see why a check, for whatever amount you think you are going to pass on, should not be here on the table now, for me to take, give to Father, and we all get the benefit of your generosity."

"You jest boy — you jest! I only have a small amount of money in the *Reichsbank* now, but I dare not touch it. Jewish accounts are being watched and frozen. If I so much as made a balance enquiry, all hell would be let loose here. One of the reasons for my survival is my great and continuing care to keep myself distant from the hawks — keeping my head well down. The rot is setting in for us. I shall never be able to get my hands on that balance, and I am glad that it is only small."

Gunther shrugged his shoulders again. "So — if all goes as you intend, how will I, or my daughters, identify ourselves to someone in Quebec or wherever in 1955? With the usual personal documents, or what?"

"Partly. I am coming to that. I have had to consider that your loyalty to me, and your father's, may become questionable in the intervening period. Thus I have provided in my will for all my assets to be given away to deserving causes in 1960 if you do not appear, or if it apparent to the trustees that you have become unworthy — by which I mean that have allied yourselves to the anti-Jewish movement internationally in such a way that your entitlement becomes morally questionable."

"If you go away now and conduct yourself as a fighter in Germany's cause — right or wrong — that will be acceptable. But if your name, or your father's, becomes associated with evil, my trustees will take note and act accordingly. Also, in this vicious age, I have had to consider that you may be forced to part with this information unwillingly. Suppose you displease someone senior to you, and they submit you to some form of forceful interrogation? It was in yesterday's paper — several *polizei* in Bremen arrested for helping a Jewish family. Are *Luftwaffe* pilots more treasured than Bremen policemen? Supposing your connection to me was discovered?"

"God forbid," said Gunther feelingly.

"Much that God forbids is happening now," said his grandfather. "Let me tell you what you must do. My friends in Canada, or their successors, will place a classified for sale advertisement in all German national newspapers. It has already been composed. It will appear on the Saturday following your birthday in 1955, so it is easy to remember. It will contain information that will relate to me, and if you, or your father or mother, look through the columns, you will recognize an obvious connection. A method of contact will be offered. Just follow it up as required. You will not be able to find out in advance what the connections will be, and that is my protection against you sharing the information with anyone else in the meantime. Even if you were forced to tell someone about the ad, they would not know what to look for. Do you understand?"

Gunther nodded slowly in resignation.

"One other thing you must know before you go," said Kurt. "I bought this *Uhland* Estate in 1929, doing so in your father's name, but without his knowledge. It is his — not mine, and he can come and do as he wishes with it all as soon as he likes. I thought at the time that it would make a nice country hotel. He may agree." He reached across to open a drawer in the table and took out a large envelope, handing it to Gunther. "Here are the deeds and other necessary documentation. I have a contract with a property management company in Celle — *Schwabl und Eppelsheimer* — for the administration of the estate, including the collection of rents of two farms. The contract with them has just been renewed and has another year to run. The estate is profitable, and they hold the funds that accrue after settling the standard expenses, including the wages of my housekeeper and gardener here. We have an annual audit and they pay the agreed balance to us. I have purposely always done business with them at a distance, using a company address in Hamburg. They have proved trustworthy hereto."

"This will now be your father's business. In that envelope are the authorities necessary for him to take over. Reassure him that there is no Jewish connection apparent in the ownership. Tell him also that some valuable things I own are here for him — particularly an original manuscript of my friend Richard Strauss Der Rosenkavalier. I shall not send anything with you now for obvious reasons, but let your father know that there are things here that he has always cherished."

Gunther looked at him in astonishment, falling silent again. Then: "You say you are on your way. Where to grandfather?"

"Best if you do not know — for now at least. Who knows what the future is going to bring, for me or for you. It could be that if I am granted another five years of life we could meet again. At least I shall know where to look for you."

Gunther was still puzzled. "But with the current rounding up of the Jews in the cities, and with all the indignities they are being subjected to, how do you manage to travel without a problem. How can you possibly leave the country?"

"I come and go as I like. It is a simple but effective deceit. For some years I have known, just as a good friend, one of the Lutheran pastors in Celle. He is sympathetic — not only to my problem — but to all Jews in the town. He cannot say much, of course, because even

Christianity is now regarded as an irrelevance by the *Nazis*. But he has been very helpful to me. When I move about, I do so dressed as a Lutheran minister. Perhaps I do not look as obviously Jewish as many others. I am just a white haired old man. I am ignored at security points and borders. May the God of Abraham forgive me, but it has proved to be the only way."

They stood up and Gunther reached for his overcoat. Kurt said: "You will have to remember what I have told you, and leave that information with your daughters somehow in case anything should happen to you. Writing may be dangerous so find another intelligent way. Your father should be told of our conversation in full. Otherwise I suggest you keep it all very quiet. What year?"

"1955 — the Saturday following my birthday."

"Where?"

"German national newspapers – for sale classified advertisements."

"Do you trust your wife?"

"Yes — but I shall tell her nothing of this. I should admit to you that she knows nothing of my part Jewish ancestry. At the time we were courting, when I had come down from university, father insisted that I offer her a slightly different version of our family history than the true one. That was, as we agreed, a protection for him and Mother, as well as for me. We have stuck to that. As things are, it is unlikely that my daughters will ever know the truth of you and our relationship. I say that with some sadness Grandfather, but we must survive. Just one dangerous revelation from somewhere could lead to disaster, and we cannot all move around dressed as Lutheran ministers. Perhaps in time it will be possible from me to tell my daughters of 1955, but not yet, and I shall conceal the Jewish connection."

"Well, it is in your hands now. I pray that you all live on so that you can enjoy the benefits."

They made their way down to the hall and shook hands deliberately. The practical and businesslike attitudes that had dominated their conversation were now replaced with emotion. The love between them became the principal focus at this moment of parting. Kurt drew his grandson to him. Both were breathless with soft sadness. As Gunther drew himself away and turned to leave, without a backward glance, he raised a gloved hand to his moist eyes.

Moments later the *Oberleutnant* was driving along the darkened tree-lined track going to the river road, and Kurt was back in his library. He lit a second oil lamp, and placed more wood on the fire. A cupboard by the door produced a glass and a decanter of brandy. He poured generously. From the drawer in the table he took a handwritten copy of a letter he had written and posted long before. He returned to his chair, turning slightly as he sat to get the maximum benefit of the light from the re-awakened fire. He read the letter, dated March 1935, to an address in London, and written in English:

> My Dear Eli,
> This brings you my most grateful sentiments and replies to your letter received yesterday. My stay with you and your kind wife brought me much joy and I shall have very happy memories of the visit. Particularly, I am happy that, with your help and the cooperation of the Board of Deputies in London, I have been able to set up a trust that will hopefully be the means of enabling me to pass on some wealth to my grandson and his children.
> As I am sure you and all your charming friends are aware, we are going through difficult times in Germany these days. For me there is the unusual problem of family loyalty, or the possible lack of it. The problem here is that loyalties have become unpredictable, and the emerging hysteria transcends traditional blood ties. I intend purposefully to deceive my son, and grandson, concerning the location of my assets and related matters for the time being. Locations and names will be known only to me and your board. I shall be telling my family that

the focus for the investments has been Canada, which is untrue of course. I am writing to the Synagogue there, where I have connections, to warn them that an approach could be made to them, and, if so, they are to ignore it. My family know nothing of my association with you personally, or of your help to me in arranging the legalities of the trust. I am comforted to learn that the funds I left you to cover the cost will prove adequate.

It is my intention to move to England once I have closed down my affairs here. I shall be in contact with you on my arrival, and look forward to a continuing association.

Yours affectionately,

Kurt lay back again, sipping his brandy — thoughtful. Then he offered the letter to the flames in front of him, releasing it as it caught fire. Within seconds it was ash. Then he moved a dining chair to the table, brought paper, pen, a glass inkwell, and a blotting pad from a cabinet drawer at the back of the library, moved the lamp closer, and wrote another letter.

My Dear Son Johann,

I write this to you within minutes of having said goodbye to Gunther, and you will already have in your hands the documentation necessary to take over this estate. I have no doubt that you will be here shortly to take charge. It has the makings and location of a fine hotel. We have a management contract with *Schwabl und Eppelsheimer* in Celle, who have administered the estate since 1935, a necessary arrangement since I have often been absent, and will be away for a while now as Gunther will have told you. I have found this firm trustworthy and recommend that you continue to retain them until the time for change becomes appropriate.

I am leaving this letter in the front cover of *Der Rosenkavalier* on the bookshelves, where I know you will find it. I am well aware of the love you have for this work, and I know that — once you are here — it will not be long before you seek out this original edition and relish the handwriting of my friend the composer. You always have, and I know that it is the obvious place to leave a note that you are sure to find. The promise that I have given you over the years that it would eventually be yours is now fulfilled.

There are uncertain times ahead as we all know, and I think it appropriate just to repeat to you that, in case there was any misunderstanding, you should seek, with Gunther and your granddaughters, to access my considerable assets elsewhere by examining the classified for sale advertisements in the columns of German national newspapers on the Saturday following Gunthers birthday (August 16th) in the year 1955. Do not forget. You will find one that obviously relates to our family, but will not be evident to anyone else. It will contain a contact procedure.

Affectionately,

Kurt returned to his fireside chair, warmed his brandy glass between his palms, and dozed in the warmth.

The next morning Gunther made the long drive to Munich to report to his father and mother on his meeting with his grandfather. He found them at the hotel that was the center of their local empire. For privacy, they moved away from the busy reception area to find a distant table on the enclosed veranda. It had been three months since they had seen their son, who had been immersed in Luftwaffe training, becoming familiar with new aircraft and equipment. They telephoned his wife in nearby Augsburg, sending a car to collect her and her daughters. They would lunch together, but the table talk in their presence would not include some of the topics about to be discussed.

Johann called for white wine and three glasses. When it had been served he sat back and looked at his son expectantly. "So — how is the old man? You kept yourself safe?"

"Yes. There was nothing about the visit that worried me seriously. It is a very quiet spot. I am sure that no-one saw me coming or going, and there was no reason for anyone to be curious." He put both his palms to his chest. "This uniform helps. It gives legitimacy to everything. People respect it. Yes — he is well, considering his age, and very clear in his mind still."

"What was the rush — why the hurry?"

"He is leaving Germany."

"Good," said his father.

His mother said: "He can get out safely?"

Her son nodded. "He believes so He has obviously made practical plans. His money opens doors for him and gives him influence. He knows — as we do — that it has to be now or never."

She said: "How will he go?"

"Dressed as a Lutheran parson, he says, but as to the route and timing, he was a bit secretive."

"Why the urgency for seeing you?"

"His money. He explained to me that he has invested most of it abroad. He says that he saw the writing on the wall with the Jewish question at least eight years ago, and moved his wealth into safer areas. He was probably right. Canada of all places though."

His father was astonished and put his wine glass down. "Canada? Why so far?"

Gunther shrugged. "The good news for you is that he bought the estate near Celle in your name. He says, and I agree with him, that it would make a fine hotel. He says that the documentation was prepared in such a way that no Jewish involvement is evident, and that you can go and take over when you like." He reached into his briefcase and produced the package of document given to him by his grandfather the night before.

His father said: "Well — I think it would be very risky to go there for the time being and claim it, whatever he says. I think I shall deal with it at a distance until things become safer. We have managed to protect ourselves very well within the areas where we have influence, and where we have earned respect and trust, but to go beyond into the unknown seems to me to be dangerous."

His wife nodded. "This Canada business. We will be able to recover the money from there?"

"Yes," said Gunther, "but not until 1955. He has made up his mind that there is going to be uncertain times ahead in Europe, so, whatever arrangements he has made, he is keeping them to himself. He would not tell me."

"1955 — Canada? Whatever possessed him?" said his father, putting both hands to his forehead.

"He says that it will be safer that way. Perhaps he is right."

His mother said: "So we wait until 1955. Then what?"

"There will be a small advertisement appearing in all the German national newspapers on the Saturday following my birthday in that year. It will make mention of family things that will be known to us, but would not mean anything to anyone else — so he says. There will be reply procedure that we have to follow up. Whoever does follow it up — you, me, my daughters if I eventually put them in the know — would have to identify themselves as being from the original Feldman family. Then the investments revert to us."

"Any of us?" asked his father.

"Apparently. He believes that, because of my age, it is more likely to be me than either of you. If we are all still about then we share it I suppose."

"His idea about including material in the advertisement that would be familiar to us is a fair one — but what, if anything happened to us, would be the destiny of the unclaimed estate?"

"Charity. The executors have been given instructions to that effect."

His mother said: " Not a happy alternative, but all will be well if you live on Gunther. For me and your father it does not matter. More wealth is always welcome, but we really have nothing to complain of, and neither have you, because we have always seen to it that you have everything you need. And as for your grandfather, we should not be sorry that he is leaving. But it is shame that it has to be that way. If things had been different, he could have had a home here."

Johann turned to look at her, wine glass poised between the linen-covered table and his lips. "Between us, that is a proper sentiment. But we must never express it in the hearing of anyone else. This is the new Germany. We are part of it and must thrive within it. His destiny must remain his own affair."

The trio fell silent, looking thoughtfully out over the hillside below, shrouded with the mist of winter — each in their own way accepting the reality of the situation, but sad that it should be.

2

1939

Heinrich Schwabl was the Celle executive who administered the Uhland Estate. The business of *Schwabl und Eppelsheimer* was wide ranging, including property sales and rentals, and maintenance work. This contract had proved to be a valuable one for them over the last four years. People from Hamburg visited it from time to time, and, although their business relationship was a distant one, the clients appeared happy with the way things had been looked after for them locally.

It was Heinrich's custom to go out to go out to the big house once a month and take the wages for the housekeeper and the gardener, at the same time making a note of anything that should be dealt with, usually as a result of their reports. He was beginning to be a little puzzled. The housekeeper told him that it was now eight months since the principal gentleman from Hamburg, who came regularly to stay, had actually made an appearance. Contract renewal was not yet due and Heinrich was custodian of the estate's funds, which were healthy, so there was no great worry. However, he thought he would make contact with the owners in Hamburg just to ensure that things were as they should be.

Not least of his concerns was the developing international situation. As a 33-year-old, he had for some time now been an army reservist, being called away often for training. He, like thousands of others, was liable to be called up to help Germany pursue its wider ambitions. He was expecting the summons at any time. Because of his age he had not been amongst the first to be recruited, but there was a need for good leaders — and his rank of *Leutnant* had been confirmed. His somewhat more mature partner would remain at home to run their business, and Heinrich intended that he should leave his side of things tidy.

Normally he corresponded with Hamburg, but he tried telephoning on this occasion to get a more prompt result to his enquiries. The telephonist who answered said that she knew nothing of *Rettburg* Shipping, but confirmed that there had been a number of company offices in that building until recently. Many had been required to move elsewhere because the building was close to the river in the city center, and that area had now become an enclosed and secure Kriegsmarine base. No — she was sorry that she had no forwarding address.

Heinrich went out to the big house. He was respected there as the substitute authority for all things if the landlord was not present. Thus he was able to ask the housekeeper if she knew anything about the relocation of her employers. This simple lady knew nothing. When Heinrich told her that he would be called away to assist the war effort, and that he ought to check over the house and its security in case anything needed doing, she readily agreed. Would her wages still be paid on time? Certainly, Heinrich told her. Everything would remain as normal as far as she was concerned.

She left him to his own devices, and he gave himself a tour. The ground floor was predictably social — lounges, a dining room, hallways and passages, and a large kitchen. He ventured to the first floor and quickly found himself in the library. This was obviously filled with bookshelves, but the presence of other furnishings indicated that it was also a place where people relaxed — in front of an open fire when it was lit, ate if they wanted to on a magnificent table, and wrote as well as read. The large bureau attested to that. Electricity had not — as he knew — reached this outlying property yet, but this room was well-equipped with oil lamps, and comfortably carpeted. He felt entitled to extend his search beyond the casual, going into the drawers of tables and cabinets. He learned much, making penciled notes on a pad from his briefcase. His intentions were honest, he told himself. He should be able to contact his clients and the information should be here somewhere that would enable him to do so.

He browsed the bookshelves, admiring the collection of classics that ran to several thousands. One section was dedicated to music — the biographies of famous composers. In this corner there was a gramophone topped with the standard brass horn, and, close to it, a section of shelving containing neatly filed records in their sleeves. There must have been at least three hundred. His eye was drawn to the cupboard above the records — glass fronted, and containing assembled and bound papers laid on their sides. He reached for them and looked at the covers. One was a hand-written sheaf of manuscript, probably fifty pages thick — a confusion of musical notation with corrections. He opened the front cover. Facing him was a letter written by 'Father' whoever he was, and addressed to a Johann.

What he read paralyzed him, first with embarrassment, and then with wickedness. He copied the letter. Who knew what the future was to bring? A glorious Germany certainly, but who would be surviving to enjoy the prosperity and comfort? Was there indeed a Jewish connection here? How could he take advantage? He thought hard. Now would not be the time to do anything. They were making money out of this estate after all. He could reasonably deny knowing more now than he had fifteen minutes ago. He would hold onto the knowledge.

What if all these descendants were to be removed from being? It was a long time until 1955, but he would still be about. There would be an ad. to watch for. If someone claimed successfully then that would be that, but he would find out and be ready to step in. He knew which paper to target. He could pick out any probables and get in touch with them saying that his name was Feldman.

In one cupboard he found a small wooden chest. It was locked, but he now knew where a little store of keys was, in a small bureau drawer. One of them fitted. These were diaries evidently. His casual first examination, and the realization that they told the story of his client, the landlord here, led to a determination to read them through. He took the chest home with him. Now he knew for certain that there was a Jewish connection here. It was all interesting. Too interesting. He was shocked by some of the revelations. Respect transformed itself first into disbelieving affront, then into hate, and then into a determination to seek revenge.

Over the course of the next two days Heinrich methodically made a record of as much as he could garner from the library and its storage. Intelligent deduction enabled him to piece together a coherent history of the Feldman family. He took nothing, knowing that at any time this Johann could turn up and take over. Business is business after all.

1940

There had been a thoughtful mood in Gunther's mess lately. Gone was the noisy bravado and back-slapping. The movement of *Jagdgeschwader 78* south into France, to a newly constructed airfield near Amiens, had followed weeks of uninterrupted glory. Rarely had these fighter pilots fought over the same terrain twice. In fact, rarely had they fought in a serious way. The ill-prepared defenses of Holland, Belgium, and France, had caved in before the overwhelming weight of Germany's armor. The *Fuhrer* had graced Paris with his personal presence, insisting that the French surrender be signed in the same railway carriage that had witness the formalization of Germany's defeat in 1918.

At the time of the euphoria in Germany after the fall of France, these pilots had yet to confront serious challenges. Their principal activity had been support of their ground troops, and they had encountered very little opposition in the air. Throughout this glorious advance, *JG78* had lost no pilots — two aircraft, yes, victims of lucky anti-aircraft fire — but no pilots. Both had managed to get to ground safely.

Then the shock. Then the emergence of stark reality — real opposition. Over the course of July, the *Luftwaffe* had been busy, crossing the Channel with the intention of letting England know who's boss. It had not worked out quite that way. From the start, with mine laying and convoy intercepting operations, and ventures to well-defended ports including Dover and Portsmouth, it had been plain that this enemy was not to be casually dealt with. He had the advantage of fighting over his own territory, and appeared to have an uncanny knowledge of where and when the *Luftwaffe* would appear. Gunther and his friends had seen considerable damage done to port installations, ships sunk, walls crumbling, and fires burning, but the resistance, if anything, had amplified rather than diminished.

In mid-August, the squadron had been assigned to bomber escort duty — an operation that had sent 150 *Dorniers* and *Heinkels* on a mission to raid the Thames estuary, pushing through to the east side of London. This raid, and others directed elsewhere in England on the same day, had led to a loss of no less than 75 German aircraft, many of them fighters. In the days preceding this adventure, a message had been circulated throughout the *Luftwaffe* bases, congratulating them on their invincibility, and urging them on confidently to greater glories. It had come from Hermann Goering, the *Luftwaffe* commanding general. It occupied pride of place on the mess anteroom notice board. The first attitudes to it had been celebratory, but now there was cynicism.

Adler Tag — Eagle's Day — August 13th, 1940, had been the target date for the *Fuhrer's* invasion of England. Now it was deferred, and his pilots — more than most — knew why. Substantial invasion forces had been accumulated at French channel ports, but it was now realized that they would not make it across this narrow stretch of water in the teeth of such determined opposition.

Twenty seven bombers were missing from yesterday's raiding. Many others had returned, but damaged, some severely, and bringing back with them maimed and seriously injured crews. Photographic evidence and post-flight debriefing offered some compensations because it was clear that London had suffered considerable damage and fires were still burning there, but the fliers were less than jubilant. In the last month the enemy had shown that he had teeth and was prepared to bite. Generally, the more maneuverable and faster fighter aircraft had better survival chances, but they had been warned that they must stay close to the vulnerable bombers on future missions. It had been too easy for them to remain at a safe height. The resent of the bomber crews at the lack of close support had already communicated itself to fighter squadrons. Where once there had been a collective sense of unified purpose, now there was recrimination.

It was seven in the evening of September 17th that *JG78* had its briefing and went out to its freshly prepared fighters. Gunther led his wing of three, and they rendezvoused with their assigned bomber squadron over Dunquerque, moving to take up protective positions ahead of, and above, their slower colleagues. The first sixty miles was reassuringly placid, a mere station keeping activity, with radios silent. Then, as usual, all hell let loose. From high above them enemy fighters appeared, diving at speed through the plodding bombers, unleashing cascades of cannon fire in their midst.

They headed doggedly on, with Gunther and the other 109s now moving out of line to the pre-arranged plan — stay between the enemy and the main attacking force. Easier said than done when there were so many of them, and appearing from unexpected directions. Bombers were already being damaged and several went down in flames in the Thames estuary area. The core pushed ahead valiantly. They not only had fighters to contend with now, but anti-aircraft fire from the ground, and the additional hazard of barrage balloons as they approached London.

Gunther waited for the moment of chaos that he knew would come. The moment when some of the bomber men would lose their nerve and drop their cargoes earlier than they were supposed to, turning out of line to head home when they had done so. Central London was the target, but he doubted whether many of them would reach it. Some of the fighters became detached, bravely pursuing their interceptors into the surrounding countryside. He had no idea now of the positions of his two wing men. Summonses on the radio produced indefinite responses when he found rare opportunities to use it — taking advantage of gaps in transmissions. Most of the chat anyway was a babble of excited exclamations that contributed little or nothing to furthering the business in hand.

Resignedly, he returned to the bomber fleet to take up his position over the leaders. There was flashing everywhere, and not only from the ground where bombs were now exploding. Below him to his right he saw fire, the starboard engine of a *Dornier*. As he watched, it fell out of line, losing height. He banked to the right to watch it as it headed towards the ground, fire spreading along the wing. He turned back toward his charges, opening the throttle wider to gain height again.

He knew from the curves of the river below him and from the built up conurbation with its closely latticed streets, that they were now over east London. He had just one thought — one that he knew he shared with all the German airmen about him — let's do the job and then get the hell out of here. He thought of his dear wife in distant Augsburg, enjoying the peace of an early Autumn evening, giving her love to their two cherished daughters. How terrified they would be if they could see him now.

Suddenly, cannon fire erupted — an ear-splitting chatter that drowned out the sound of the engine in front of him. The noise started behind him and moved forward. He turned his head instinctively to the left where the sound seemed to be concentrated, but saw nothing. His face was burning — pin pricks of pain. He turned his head back towards his instruments, raising his eyes to look through the screen ahead of him. Eyes? He saw nothing. He was suddenly conscious of wind, violent slipstream tearing at his helmet, chilling his nose. Why could he not see? He tore off his right glove and put his bare hand up to his face. Even with the cold wind lancing into it, he could still feel the lacerations. He put his hand forward at head height. There as no screen. It had been shot away.

Desperately he wiped his eyes. His eyes? He could not feel them — could not feel the bulge beneath his fingers, beneath the lids. Just moist stickiness. He could not see. What to do? Get back into control. I will be all right in a minute or two. This is a shock reaction. I shall be able to see again shortly. Keep the plane on an even keel. Hand on the stick. Now — feel for the familiar sounds. Engine speed about right. Flying level? Yes. He put a hand above him. The canopy of his cockpit, which should have been only six inches above his head, was gone. Around him now was the noise of rushing air. He lifted his goggles from his chest and put them on. Like everyone else he rarely wore them. They got in the way and interfered with lateral vision.

He flew on straight and level, with the engine pitch warning him if he pulled the nose up or dropped it too far. What could he do about his eyes? He had no water — nothing with which to bathe them. Several minutes passed and, as they did, the realization dawned with savage certainty — he was blind. The cannon fire of the enemy had blown away his front shield and canopy, fracturing the laminated glass that had sprayed back into his unprotected face.

He knew he must abandon the plane. How could he land it? At least he was at an altitude where a parachute jump could be made safely — somewhere around three thousand feet. He must get out. He must jump. He checked the harnesses on his shoulders and the position of the release button. One of the straps had apparently been severed, but the other was tight and intact. He hoped it would hold. Because of the howling slipstream and the close confinement of the cockpit, it was not easy to move and check everything out. Hell! So what — he had to go — now! He stood, turning as he did so, climbing up onto the seat so that he was facing aft along the fuselage. He leant forward, but could not climb any further because of gravity, weakness, and the wind. He stretched his left leg back to move the stick to the port side as hard as he could. The *Messerschmidt* obediently banked to the left. Gravity helped him now. He fell free.

1942

Kurt, his affairs in Germany wound up as far as they could be, traveled light to Brussels two days after his conversation with Gunther at Celle in November 1938. He spent one night there and then continued his journey to England via Calais. His English connections were strong, and his appeal to the authorities there to be allowed to remain was sympathetically agreed to. He had means enough to settle himself comfortable amongst the Jewish community, who treated him with generosity and respect. Having only lately celebrated his eighty-fifth birthday, he died of old age in 1942. Throughout his residence in London, then immersed — locally and distantly — in the full savagery of the war, he had no contact with family or friends outside Britain.

3

The Present

"We may have a body in the copse," said his mother bluntly down the 'phone. She had always been matter-of-fact, but this came as something of a shock — certainly more than a simple surprise. Mark put down his pen, swiveled his chair to face the window overlooking the college quadrangle, and waited for more. "I was out along the ridge with Muffin an hour ago, and he disappeared, as he usually does, to have a nose about in the thickets on the steepest part. Are you listening?"

"With rapt attention Mother."

"Well, he reappeared with something in his mouth, sort of muddy, and dropped it at my feet. I was just going to leave it, but then I noticed that it looked like to bones of two human fingers, so I stopped to have a closer look. He finds all sorts of things, usually dead birds and bony stuff that the badgers leave about, but this is a little unusual. Anyway, I think I am right, two fingers joined with a sort of cartilage at the wrist end — either human or ape, and we have had no apes here in living memory. What should I do?"

"What have you done with them?"

"Left them where they are. Should I call the police?"

Mark thought. It was Thursday afternoon. It was a twenty-mile drive, but the weekend was reasonably free.

"No mother. I'll come down on Saturday morning to have a look at them. No point in bothering anyone else for the moment. If they turn out to be bird's legs or something, then the police would not thank you for calling them in. It might be helpful if you could go back that way and pick them up — in case something wild takes a fancy to them."

"Absolutely not. They stay where they are. I did not rear a lumbering scruff of a tousle-headed son to send me on macabre errands. You come and pick them up."

Mark shrugged his shoulders. This was his formidable mother. There could be no arguing. He wondered about the likelihood of her being right about the find, and was doubtful. He said: "You have had no problems there have you? No noise? No intruders?"

"No. Nothing like that. It's on our property for one thing, quite isolated as you know, and not very tempting to trespassers or wanderers down there, so steep and so boggy at the bottom. Your father never bothered to try and tame it. He always said that even if he drained it out with ditches and things, the land would never be much use to us."

Goodbyes said, Mark rose and went across to the big window. Students were walking the paths and talking in groups, sitting on the bench-high stone base of the founder's statue. He was done for the day but there were lectures going on elsewhere in the college. The June sky was bright, the afternoon sun throwing shadows across the grass below. He thought of Muffin, the black Labrador that was now, since his father's death, his mother's principal companion. She insisted on remaining in the big old house, with its rambling grounds, in which he had spent his childhood.

Human bones in the copse? Could it be? It was certainly an inaccessible spot, about two acres of steep ground leading down to a ditch that flowed with water in the winters, covered with ferns, gorse, and thorny briars. Here and there silver birches and elder pushed their heads above the thick green undergrowth. He wondered again about his mother's judgment. Yes, probably something left by a badger. He went back to his desk. This had been an interesting diversion, but meanwhile he was a lecturer in mathematics, and there were things to do.

He called his wife Sue. She would need to know that Saturday now had more commitment to it than meeting the usual bunch of chums for a lunchtime buffet at The Crown. She was the senior nurse at one of the town surgeries. Not only would her knowledge be useful, but she had a personality that burned with curiosity, and would not take kindly to being left out of this.

They took coffee informally at Mother's kitchen table late on Saturday morning, exchanged news, and then walked together through the formal garden and out onto the ridge beyond, Muffin leading the way. They came to the fingers. Mark bent to look at them closely and then picked them up. Sue also gave them a close scrutiny, a palm raised to her right forehead to prevent a cascade of fair hair from interrupting the view. "Human fingers — definitely," she said, and lifted them from Mark's palm She flexed the joints, and examined them from all angles. "Man-sized — undamaged — probably a youngish person because the joints are still very straight. And there are no indications of anything arthritic or similar."

"How old?" asked mother, standing back in distaste.

"Who knows," said Sue. "I am not an expert, but I read in one of our textbooks once that a body left in an exposed place undisturbed loses all its flesh with decomposition within about four months in our climate, so all that is left is a skeleton after that time has elapsed. And flesh loss in an environment like this could involve other factors. Let's face it — foxes, badgers, and crows are not particular where they get their nourishment from."

Mark said: "So, it could be less than a year old. However, it could be ten years old presumably."

"Or a hundred — or more," said Sue. "One hears occasionally of mediaeval remains being uncovered. They would probably look like this. Bone is almost everlasting."

Mark turned to his mother. "One thing is certain of course. Muffin did not dig down six feet to some across a couple of fingers. He could only have found them on or close to the surface. That suggests skullduggery or accident, rather than formal burial Have you got any idea where he found them?"

She turned to wave a hand vaguely in the direction of the slope below them. "Down there somewhere. When he comes back after his explorations, he normally emerges there." She pointed with more precision at a gap in the growth about thirty yards distant.

Sue looked at Mark. "Well — he has discovered a body it seems. Sobering thought. Are you going to go down and see what you can find?"

Mark was thoughtful. Reluctant to go, but knowing that he should. He nodded. Sue said that she would stay with Mother. Muffin, an old chum of Mark's, went with him willingly, led the way to the gap, and on into the wildness of the copse. Movement here was easier for dog than man, but they made their way together down the slope, Mark kicking through the heavy undergrowth and brushing branches away from his face. Suddenly, Muffin stopped, turned to face his companion, and sat on his haunches. Behind him was a large hawthorn shrub, but where he sat was relatively clear grass-covered ground. They were about twenty yards above the bottom of the copse, and Mark could see through to a field of young green cereal, property of the neighboring farmer.

Muffin began to sniff at the ground. Mark came closer and ran his fingers through the grassy surface. He felt a sharpness in the soft damp earth. A stone? He probed, feeling something like a twig. He gripped it between thumb and finger and pulled. It came free — another finger! He stood back from the spot, a little shocked. By nature he was a calm realist, but to be this close to human remains was sobering. For several seconds he considered the angle at which the finger had lain in the shallow earth, deducing from it where the rest of the remains were likely to be. Then he retraced his steps laboriously up the slope, coming out into the open.

Sue advanced to meet him. "You've found something more?"

"Yes — another finger." He held it up. He was relieved to be back in company again.

"Police?" asked his mother, who had bent down to hold Muffin by his collar, almost as if she feared he would go on to unearth further sinister relics.

Mark, thoughtful and hesitant, looked at Sue. "What do you

think?"

She shrugged her shoulders. "If it was obviously a recently dead person, there could only be one answer to that, but I believe that whoever it is has been there for a long time, so there could hardly be any urgency about it. If we have part of a hand, then probably the rest is there as well. Why not have a search around and see what else there is before spreading the news. It may be very interesting. If it proved to be a fairly recent unexplained death, then the police would have to know — but if it turned out to be an old ploughman who died of natural causes two hundred years ago, then we are into archeology, not criminology."

Mark nodded. His mother said: "Well — as you wish, so long as you handle it all discretely. I must say I do not relish the thought of hordes of people invading our quiet." She led the way back to the house.

Equipped with rubber boots, a spade and a trowel, and some carrier bags, Mark and Sue made their way back to the copse. Some shallow work exposed the radius and ulna bones of an arm. Sue was scraping the earth away with gloved hands and exclaimed: "Good heavens — a wrist watch!" She held it up and they marveled. The leather strap was intact on one side, fitted to the lug on the watchcase. The buckle, given a light rub, showed up as brass. The glass was intact and, once rubbed clean, showed a time of 1:15. Sue put it reverently into one of the carrier bags.

They stood and considered. Mark said: "We are going about this the wrong way — working down from the top. It would be better if I dug a trench here on one side and we explore in from there." Sue nodded, and he went to work, going into the soft earth to a depth of eighteen inches over a length of about five feet.

Progressively, they worked their way gently sideways. There were remains of leather clothing, a jacket with its zip front still intact though badly rusted, and the vertebrae of the lower back and the femur. They carefully filtered each handful of earth through their fingers as they went, and another exclamation, this time from Mark, accompanied the discovery of a cluster of coins, a key ring with five keys, a metal disc, and an oblong metal plate still intact.

They were now able to distinguish how the skeleton lay and gently looked for the skull. Finding it led to the discovery of an aviator's goggles, remnants of a leather helmet, the metallic fixings that had been part of it, and some cloth-backed metallic woven badges. There was a chain round the neck, with another metal disc hanging from it.

Sue stood, hands pressed against the small of her back. "We need a break. This bending is beginning to get to me." Mark agreed. He rose from the crouch, and climbed out of the trench to stand beside her. Contemplating the remains in front of them, they had a moment of quiet respect and reverence for this man, whoever he was. Mark took the coins out of his jacket pocket, and rubbed the earth from the faces of two of them so that the design could be seen He laid them on his palm, and they both looked at them with fascination.

"Ten *Reichmarks*," read Sue. "German then."

"Yes," said Mark in a hushed voice. "Yes — and old German. They became *Deutschmarks* after the war, and then Euros of course. And the goggles — the zip-fronted boots. We know he was an airman, and he was not buried — too shallow and no laid out posture."

"No sign of bone damage or injury yet though," she said. "An escaping prisoner?"

"No — not in this much uniform. They would have taken his helmet and goggles away." Mark turned to face her. "If he fell from a plane which was blown up over here during the war, which seems the most likely explanation to me, the impact of hitting the ground would have finished him wouldn't it?"

"Certainly," Sue said. "There is no sign of a parachute or a harness. And he may have been dead before he hit the ground. If it had been a death caused by fire — burning — asphyxia, we would not know now because all the flesh and lung tissue has gone." And then, as a practical afterthought appropriate to a nurse: "What do we do then?"

"There must be more. Even if it no longer readable, he must have been carrying identification. We should know who he is if possible. The remains can be left here for the moment, because, after all, he has lain on this spot in peace for more than sixty years probably. But

I think we can take away and examine all the things we have found. Perhaps he has living relatives — a family who would like to know where he ended up."

"How old would he have been?"

"Who knows — under thirty probably."

"Well — if he had lived on he would be over ninety now," she said.

"There could have been children."

Mark stepped down into the trench again, and began to remove shallow earth from the left side of the ribs. He had to clear a wide area down to hip level, and then found what they sought, a wrapped packet made of what he knew his mother would call oil cloth — not a wallet in the usual way, but more like a tobacco pouch, about the size of a video cassette. He handed it up to his wife. "We are going to have to examine that with great care," he said. "It is going to be very fragile." She nodded, placing it gently in the carrier bag.

Mark's curiosity had gone beyond identification. "I wonder if he was armed — a pistol or something." There could be other things around.

"I think you should leave at that for the moment," said the practical Sue. "Just cover up the exposed areas again. This does not close the affair, does it. A proper burial would be appropriate at some point. We will be coming back, maybe with others once we have thought about it."

They tidied up the area and returned to the house, quietly thoughtful, Mark carrying the tools, and Sue with two carrier bags. Being aware of his mother's sensitivities, Mark put them in the back of his car. Coffee was being poured when he got back to the kitchen. His mother said: "The poor man has obviously been there since sometime in World War Two which is a sad thought." She looked at her son. "You are only thirty two, and I am not yet sixty, so neither of us are going to have much idea of how it was in those difficult times, but your grandfather has often talked about it." She paused, spoon hovering over the sugar bowl. "He has some harrowing tales to tell of German bombers over London. They did not drop much out here in the country, but we are only thirty miles from Piccadilly Circus, so some of them used to end up here. Planes go a long way in a short time. There is a veterans' club in the town where they keep memorabilia and records of that time, and they probably know where there were crashes in this neighborhood. The local paper would have archive records."

Mark pondered. Sue, holding a shortcake biscuit delicately, said: "He must have relatives. He may have had a wife. They may have children, and if they did they could still be living. Cousins?" She dipped the biscuit into her coffee — not quite so delicately.

Mark said: "There will have been some mystery amongst his family about his destiny. They will have been told that he was missing, presumed dead. Prisoners of war were repatriated eventually, but not the dead — and certainly not the lost dead like our friend."

Mother asked: "Are we going to be able to find out who he is?"

"My guess is yes," said Mark. "I have put some of his stuff in the car. We will clean it up and go through it later. There are some papers. His name will be there somewhere."

"You have left him where he was?" said mother.

"Yes, he is covered up again. At some stage we will have to formalize a burial somehow, but there will be some research to do before that can happen."

"Well," said his mother. "I am not too happy to have him there I can tell you. If I hear any moans during the dark hours I am going to be worried. Just keep your guest room free for occupation at short notice." His son looked at her anxiously, but there was a twinkle in her eye.

Later, back in their own home, they spread the contents of the carriers out on the kitchen table. Sue unfolded the oil-cloth wrapper carefully. There were papers in it, compressed and yellowed, neatly folded, but apparently intact — damp but not soaked. Watched with bated breath by Mark, she separated them. One was a stapled booklet, blue covered. It said *Flugbuch* on the front. Mark held it reverently. "It's a pilot's flight logbook." He carefully inserted a table knife between the cover and the first page, twisting it to separate them gently. Once it was half open he flattened it carefully. The printed text part of the page was in antique Teutonic script, but the name hand-written in ink on the blank center line was clear — *Oberleutnant* Gunther Muller. The date was clear also — October 1939. The page had been rubber stamped at the bottom over an unclear signature. Within its enclosing boundary circle was the *Swastika*, surmounted with an eagle, its wings spread. Alongside was another, smaller, rubber stamp — *JG78*.

"Awesome," said Mark. "Transported back to another age."

"I think we should leave it at that for the moment," the practical Sue said to him. "Don't try to separate any more pages or open the rest until it has dried out further. Even on that inside cover, some of the print is lifting off one side and transferring to the other."

He nodded. "It isn't just damp I think, but the time factor. These papers have been pressed together for so long that they are practically solidified into a single pad."

"John Shaw's expertise could be useful," said Sue. Their friend was chemistry professor at the college.

He nodded again. "He would know what to do, and I will have a word with him on Monday. Thing is — how many people do we tell about this? We have to be careful. As a discovery it is not unique, but it is unusual, and if the local or national papers got to know of it, then the whole thing would be taken out of our hands. But I am not an authority on the subject of ancient aviators, and neither are you. Perhaps we should resign ourselves to the inevitable and pass the whole thing over to experts."

"What experts?" said his wife. "We are obviously not dealing with crime here — unless you want to moralize about the war. It is clear to us already that this man Gunther Muller fell — or was blown out of — a German plane, probably during the battle of Britain that your mother was talking about. He came to earth unnoticed, dead or dying, in an isolated copse on private ground in Buckinghamshire. No so-called expert is going to arrive at a different conclusion."

"I cannot disagree with that."

"All the items we have found on him, the papers, badges, bits of remnant clothing and their metal fixings, rusted zip-fasteners and things, the coins and the keys. They are just as commonplace as protective uniform wear and pocket contents now as they were then, just less modern. We do not need to be experts to recognize a key. What we should be doing is tracing him back to his military records in Germany if that can be done, and then research his family connections. All the stuff we found should be returned to them, and they should have choices as to how his remains are to be permanently interred. They may want to take him back to Germany."

Mark nodded. "That would be true if we could find them. You are assuming, as you said earlier, that he has living relatives. He may not have. Thousands died in Germany as the war went on, particularly towards the end. Even if we were to come across records of his service career up until the time he died — and we do not know if that is going to be possible — we are unlikely to be able to trace relatives easily after such a long time."

"Well — even so," said Sue deliberately, "I think we are quite entitled to keep it to ourselves for the time being. It will be interesting to follow it all up, and I think we would be as well qualified to check it out as anyone else."

Mark raised his hands in resignation. He sat and reached for his teacup. "Okay. I'll see what I can organize with John, and mum's the word for the moment."

"You had better make the secrecy angle clear to your mother. If she were to drop a word of lament or speculation to one of her Women's Institute chums, then who knows where it would end. And the last thing we want now is stream of indelicate trespassers tramping down into the copse and wandering away with things that we have yet to find."

4

It was three weeks later when John Shaw joined Mark and Sue in their lounge for an evening conference over a glass of wine. College was now in recess and the pressure was off the academics. The original intention that John should be consulted about the recovery of the documents found on Gunther's body had, as Mark supposed it would, expanded into his full involvement in what they called 'the project.'

The internet had given them a confirmation of Gunther's identity, his operational squadron, and the date he went missing — September 17, 1940. A German website representing a group of historians who had carefully preserved the original wartime records of *Luftwaffe* operations and personnel had produced the information. Even now, so many years after the war, this group continued to seek to update their records. Many questions concerning the destiny of aviators remained unanswered. Astonishing to the trio was that fact that close to 1,000 German airmen had become missing in action during the war on all fronts — Europe, Russia, North Africa — over land and ocean, and nothing was known of their destiny to this day.

Gunther had been a fighter pilot — *Messerschmidt 109s* — and was with JG78 at the time he went missing. How he had become detached from his aircraft over Buckinghamshire would never be known, and a check through archive records in the local papers, focusing on the known date, offered no clues. If he had bailed out at seven or eight thousand feet, his damaged fighter may have flown on for as many as thirty miles before crashing.

He should have been able to parachute to safety, and would

routinely have been in harness from the moment he took off, attached to his folded 'chute. Had he parachuted down onto open ground, already injured but landing safely, discarding his harness and canopy because they impeded him, and then crawled into the copse to die? They would never know.

Sue had always liked John. To her he was the typical chemistry buff — bearded and often a little unkempt, large-handed, corduroy jacketed and suede shoed. His merriment was infectious. She and Mark joked often about the 'fragrances' that John took everywhere with him — remnants of his laboratory activities. He was a bachelor. Not least of the valuable contributions he had already made to their researches was his fluent German. Neither Mark nor Sue were strong in this area, but were already studying it keenly, their enthusiasm awakened by the prospect of the continued ferreting that obviously lay ahead of them.

Most of the finds on the body in the copse had been put to one side, safely stored. Nothing more would be learned for the moment from the badges, coins, keys and the rest. They had all held them and examined them with awe, and eventually, they knew, it would be proper for them to be passed on elsewhere. The obvious important focus had been on the documents. John had taken them away with him, dried them out, in a desiccation chamber as he described it, separated them, and translated them. Each was now enclosed in its own clear plastic folder. He laid the collection on the coffee table in two piles.

"Utterly fascinating," he said, putting his briefcase down beside him. "The chaps in Germany will be interested in all this eventually. They told me that very little personal documentation of this time remains. It appears that as the end of the war approached, any surviving aviators destroyed their papers believing that they could be incriminating if they were taken prisoner. They may have presumed some lenience if their captors were to be us or the Americans, but the Russians were seen as less predictable and a more sinister threat to personal survival."

"Did you tell them what we had?" asked Mark.

"No. I did not mention any finds, and neither did I mention the discovery of a body. My exchanges of Email with them were rather more abstract. Finding out about Gunther was easy because all the aviators — destiny known or not — are listed on their site. You just go into an alphabetical index and scroll the names. There are thousands of them, but there was only one Gunther Muller amongst the missing, and he must be our man." He leant forward and pointed at the folders. "These are separated into two sets — the originals, and the translations. I did not bother to go right through the log book, which is just a record of when he took to the air, but I have been carefully though everything else." He sat back, picking up his wineglass.

Sue reached for the first folder. "So this is a driving license." She read it through and reached for the original to see how it compared with John's tidy word processor text. "It gives a personal address — 26 Ludwigstrasse, Augsburg. And his signature again." She passed the folder to Mark beside her.

Next was a personal letter. She looked at John. "Headed notepaper in the original?" He nodded. She read: "*Friesinger Waldhaus.* Presumably the names printed beneath the address are the owners — Johann and Inge Muller. So — Gunther's parents." She looked at the men in turn, and then lowered her head to quote. "Dear Gunther. We were very pleased to receive your letter yesterday, and glad to know that there is so much confidence in your squadron. Our newspapers here are full of the wonderful achievements of all our services, and there have been great celebrations following the news of the fall of France. The hotel had been very busy for many days now, with parties, particularly for those of our fighting heroes who have had an opportunity to return to their homes in this region for some leave. We hope very much that we shall be able to parade you proudly when you are able to come home, and you may be sure that your favorite *rostbratwurstl* will be here to greet you. Feel free to bring companions with you if perhaps they live too far away to return to their own homes."

"Your father says this is a wonderful time for the new Germany, compared with the miseries that we all had to suffer in the last war, and the injustices that followed. How wonderful that the *Fuhrer* has been able to show these arrogant foreigners that we are not to be trifled with. There are going to be glorious times ahead. We have no doubt that you are getting plenty of news from Gisella at home in Augsburg. We bring her and girls here often as you know, believing that she likes to be in our company when you have to absent for a long time. She knows, as do you, that here is always comfort and a welcome for her here."

"We pray for your safety, and we want you to be careful to preserve yourself sensibly. It looks as though our great new nation is going to be able to have things its own way, but please be careful to be sober and sensible with all your flying. As your father says, you are there to kill, but not be killed. Your affectionate parents."

She laid the letter down in front of her. They all remained silent for a long moment, overwhelmed with the gravity of the words — all aware of the delicacy and intensity of those distant sentiments, and all aware that history was to deny them.

Sue picked up the next. "Another letter. This one written by the father apparently, Johann Muller. Dear Gunther. Your mother told me that you were able to telephone yesterday and she has passed on the news of your achievements. We are very proud to learn that your score of kills now qualifies you for a decoration. We look forward to hearing the news. Yet another reason for celebration here for your family and friends She tells me you asked about Celle and whether we had been up there. As she told you, the answer is no. I consider it rather dangerous to venture into that territory for the time being I am happy to remain at a distance. I am assuming that your grandfather did not let anyone up there know where to find me, because it's now more than a year since you met him and I have heard nothing. No matter. When Germany is celebrating its victories and the fighting is over, I shall still have the legal proof of my ownership of the *Uhland* Estate there, and, who knows, you may want to settle there with your own family."

"One thing I did do," the letter went on, "and that was to send one of my trusted people up there to recover a particularly valuable heirloom that I was anxious about — the original manuscript of Richard Strauss's *Der Rosenkavalier* that you said had been left there for me. My man, also with my authority, looked around for anything else that could be of value for us, and I now have a chest of papers that your grandfather obviously intended I should find. They include his diaries for most of this century. Unfortunately there is so little time now with the war and trying to keep our business going, that I cannot enjoy the quiet to go through everything, but one day I shall. Meanwhile all those papers are in my security closet, that recess at the back of the paneling behind the door leading to the old brewery, where you once loved to hide."

"This letter brings my best wishes for your continuing good luck and safety. We have a noble cause, and it is in your trust. Your affectionate father."

"That," said John, " is a formidable link with the past, is it not? I wonder if that manuscript is still in its hiding place? It must be worth thousands." Mark topped up the wineglasses. John said: "There is a third letter — the next one down — from the wife."

Sue reached for it. "26 Ludwigstrasse, Augsburg — so, the same address as on his driving license — My Dear Gunther. Those were two days of joy, not just for me, but also for Helga and Lise. We were so proud of you, taking us into town in your uniform, so that all our friends could see you in all your smartness, and — a gap there John?"

He nodded. "If you look at the original you can see that it was just not possible to separate the sheet tidily. And her handwriting is less clear than his mother's and father's, more of a scrawl, and it has the flowery embellishments of the old German that do not add to clarity. But her signature is clear at the bottom."

"Yes," said Sue. "Gisella. So she was Gunther's wife."

Mark said: "Do we know how old Gunther was?"

John reached into the folders, producing one and passing it across. "His service identity card — born August 17, 1916."

"So the remains we uncovered were of a man of twenty-four."

"That's right." John nodded again.

"So," said Sue, " what else John?" She reached over to pick up the remaining folders.

"Nothing else of any factual interest, but they are fascinating even so. Two cancelled railway tickets, a receipted bill for a dinner in *Dusseldorf,* and a scribbled pencil note that reads "see you in the mess at ten o'clock — call Hermann on — and it gives a telephone number."

Mark sat back, folded his arms, and closed his eyes in thought. "Well, all of this is over sixty years old. So what are we left with? The grandfather mentioned has obviously long gone. The father was Johann and owned a hotel in Munich, where he lived with his wife Anna. The wife Gisella lived in Augsburg, wherever that is."

"About fifty miles away from Munich to the west," said John.

Mark mused on. "Well, she, at the time of her letter, may have been about twenty two, a little younger than her husband we can suppose. They evidently had two daughters, who were old enough to appreciate their father's presence on leave, so were they three and four years old? It is likely. If so they were born in about 1936, so they could still be living."

"Certainly," said Sue. "They would be in their late sixties."

"And they would be contactable," said John. "Grandmothers themselves by now. Hey — wouldn't they love to know about all this." He waved an arm across the folder on the table. "What do you two sleuths see as the next step then?"

Sue said: "It does seem rather obvious. An advertisement or two in German newspapers – maybe focusing on that Bavarian region." The men both nodded.

John rose and said: "Good — well, keep me briefed, and let me know if I can contribute further." He drained his glass, grabbed his much used and tattered briefcase, and departed.

Over the next couple of days, Mark and Sue gave thought to an ad. in the German press. Had the daughters survived the war? If they were still alive had they remained in Germany? Had they grown up in the Munich area? Had they migrated to other German provinces as the result of marriages? In the end they decided to try a local regional paper to start with. They thought it likely that the young girls would stay close to the place of their birth.

Their choice was the *Bavarische Volkszeitung*. It read, in John's polished German: "Contact is sought with Helga and/or Lise, granddaughters of Johann and Anna Muller, late of the *Friesinger Waldhaus*, and daughters of Gunther and Gisella Muller, late of Augsburg. We have information relating to their father. Reply to Box number."

The internet provided the means to place the ad. and it duly appeared in three consecutive July editions. They did not expect a reply. Looming over the whole of their thinking was the time lapse — over sixty years. None of the family may have survived the war. Did they read the newspapers? Were their circumstances and their family history well enough known to third parties who could draw the ad. to their attention? An air of fatalism hung over their household, but they waited patiently.

Then, after three weeks, a reply arrived, forwarded by the newspaper. It was in a neatly written envelope, carefully sealed. A single sheet of notepaper bore the brief letter. A call to John produced an instant translation: "84 Regenerstrasse, Halle. Dear Advertiser. I am the daughter of of Gunther Muller. I can be contacted at this address and will be interested to hear your information." It was signed Lise Bormann. There was a telephone number.

Both Mark and Sue had been working hard at their German and were pleased with the result, but they were far from ready to risk a distant conversation. They considered when they could make a journey together, identifying an available week when Sue could be away from her surgery duties. John stepped into the breach again to make contact with Lise Bormann. He rang her, mentioning that the remains of her father had been found in England, and that some of the possessions and documents found with him would be returned to her. Could Mark and Sue Woodford bring these things to her, and discuss what she may want to do with the remains?

She agreed without any hesitation, John said, and an appointment was made. They were to go to her house. In conversation she mentioned that her married sister Helga lived in Stuttgart. She would be getting in touch with her, and would arrange for her to come to Halle to meet the Woodfords. Her manner, said John, was a mixture of pleasure and sadness — consolation that her father had at last been found, and a grateful reaction to the efforts of distant English people to contact her in such a generous way.

Another week had to pass before Mark and Sue were to leave, taking their car across the Channel by ferry, and then the drive to Halle. They had not expected any more replies to the ad., so the arrival of another envelope surprised them. It was from a law firm in Celle, headed notepaper and very formal. "This replies to your advertisement in the *Augsburgher Volkszeitung.* Acting on behalf of clients, we request that you contact us with information concerning the affairs of Gunther Feldman, formerly of Celle." Nothing more than that.

Sue said to Mark: "What on earth can that be about? Someone chasing him for debt after all these years? An aggrieved relative?"

"Well — whatever. But I think it best to ignore it for the time being. Our proper route to make a connection was via his daughters, and we have succeeded in that. Our concern must remain limited to the body and the things found with it. If other complications appear, then they become the business of the daughters. We will give the letter to them."

"Interesting though," said Sue. "Anyone reading our ad. is going to assume that it has German origins, someone just down the road. They will not know that there is an English connection."

"True," said Mark.

Their next agreed task was to tidy up the mess they had left in the copse at the time of the discoveries. They went together, with Muffin in company, to clear up the area. They carefully removed the whole skeleton, now separated into many sections, and placed it carefully in a small but respectable wooden chest that Mark had found in a secondhand furniture shop. It seemed pointless to look for anything resembling a full-sized coffin. They tidied up the site, finding nothing else to add to the original discoveries. Their garage was to become Gunther's temporary resting place. Mother was pleased that her uninvited copse guest was leaving, but expressed surprise at the choice of his new home, temporary or not. "Could you not have made a more delicate arrangement?" she asked her son.

"Not important," he told her. "After all, the only difference between what is left of him and an urn of cremated ashes, is the minor one of form, and people leave those urns around everywhere. He will not mind."

"Are you going to take him to Germany with you?"

"No mother. That would be unwise for several reasons. Apart from our simple human reaction to finding him of having respect for his remains, he means nothing to us personally. Imagine how crass it would be for me to turn up at someone's house with their father rattling about in a wooden box? Not only that, but I imagine the Customs on either side of the Channel would have some interesting thoughts about who he is, how he died, and where he is going. And bear in mind that, as we have kept all this very quiet, we have not obtained the necessary authorities to move him. That will have to happen later."

5

So — now they must go off to Germany. Politely, they asked John if he would like to go with them, but he declined. He had many other things to do, he said. They knew he was anxious to be helpful, but did not want to interfere. They wondered about their ability to communicate. They had both waded into the German language with enthusiasm, and had heads full of phrases and words, but they knew they were far from the stage when they could carry on complex conversations. However, they knew much more than they had a month ago, and it probably would help a little. After all, their mission was a simple one — to let the relatives of a dead airman know that his body had been found, and hand over his possessions. They had arranged to be at the Bormann house at ten o'clock, two days ahead, and thought that they could be on their way home again by lunchtime. It was play it by ear. Sue had a week's leave, so one option would be to look at the Rhine Valley on their way home.

It was a long drive to Halle. Anticipating this, and expecting to be tired after the journey, they had an overnight stop in a roadside hotel just west of the town. Next morning, they found their way without difficulty to the house of Lise Bormann. It was terraced, small and tidy, but they could not park outside in this busy street, and had to walk nearly a quarter of a mile, carrying all the things that would need to be handed over.

They were met at the front door by a cheerful man — sixty plus and portly. His greeting was in German, but when it was instantly apparent that they were hesitant, he changed over to English that he obviously spoke fluently. His brief explanation for this, when they showed pleasant surprise, was that he had worked for some years in an American military base in the vicinity earlier in his life. He invited them in and led the way to the back room. Here two smiling ladies of mature age were standing to greet them, both gray-haired, slim and neat. He introduced them as Lise, his wife, and her sister Helga. He said his name was Helmut. They were invited to sit.

Mutual interest was apparent. Neither side had known what to expect of this encounter. The two ladies looked at their guests searchingly. One could almost read their minds. News had arrived out of the blue concerning a cherished father who had left their lives in their childhood, never to be seen again until these English people had made their discoveries. They were now to hear about them. It would be an emotional moment. Their friendliness was spontaneous and warm, but they were in suspense and it showed. For Mark and Sue there was also a sense of gravity and responsibility, both appreciating the need to be gentle in their descriptions, and generous in their thinking.

Helmut was talkative. Both ladies had halting English, but where problems of understanding arose, he intervened to clarify. He told Mark and Sue that he was the head waiter in one of the town's principal hotels. It became a warm and sympathetic meeting. To start with they politely exchanged pleasantries about their visit, the weather, and Helga's journey from Stuttgart. Then, over coffee, they came to the point of the meeting.

"You have some information for us about our father?" Lise said.

Because they had obviously taken and instant liking to the trim and comely Sue, Mark gestured to her to start the explanations. "Yes, we know that your father was Gunther Muller, and we know that he was a pilot in the *Luftwaffe* during the war. Evidently he became separated from his aircraft over England sometime, probably when the raids were being concentrated on London. His remains were discovered about a month ago in a copse of wild ground about forty miles from London that belongs to Mark's mother. This is a very inaccessible area, rather wild and overgrown, and far from any roads or public places. It should not surprise us that it lay there undiscovered for so long."

Helga asked: "Are you certain that it is him?"

"As certain as we can be. He was carrying documents that we have brought with us to give you — a service identity card, driving license, and some personal letters, evidently from your grandparents who had a hotel in Munich at that time, and one from his father mentioning your grandfather and his estate at Celle."

The sisters looked at each other in surprise, but for the moment said nothing.

"Where are his remains now?" asked Helmut.

Mark knew he had to answer this delicately. They were hanging on his every word. "He had evidently fallen into his resting place. He had obviously not been buried in a formal way. Over time he had subsided into the soft ground on a steep slope, so that some parts of him were more than a foot down in the earth. It was clear from finds close to the surface that he was a German aviator. In other words, it was quickly evident that he was a victim of a war that had taken place many years ago, and there would be no requirement for us to involve the police." Nodding towards Sue, he said: "We personally exhumed him very gently, finding as we did so a number of things including his badges, some money, keys, pieces of his flying uniform including his goggles, and a waterproofed wrapper with documents in it. His complete remains have now been boxed with care, and, subject to your instructions and wishes, remain with us for the moment. Sue and I have kept this whole matter very secret. Until now it has only been known to four people."

His briefcase lay on the floor beside him. He reached into it and produced the folders of the original documents and neatly packed plastic bags with the other items. He put them on the coffee table between them. The three Germans gazed at them spellbound. It seemed that they were hesitant even to pick them up. Sue took the initiative, unzipping the bag with the badges in it, including the pilot's wings, the identity tag, and the rank panels. Because of their non-ferrous metal content they had survived the burial very well. The bunch of keys on its ring was separately bagged and Sue opened it, placing them on the table top.

Lise picked up the wings reverently. Helga leaned close to her to get a better view, adjusting the spectacles on her nose. They were silent in awe and emotion.

Helmut was rather more practical and less personally involved. He reached for the document folders and browsed them. After a quick examination he asked Lise, with surprise in his voice: " Did your grandparents own the *Friesinger Waldhaus?"*

She looked at him, and then at Helga. "We think perhaps they did. We used to go there as small children, and that is where they lived. We have always supposed that they sold it, or lost possession of it after the war. Whatever — there was nothing there for us. No documents, and they left us no information of course."

Mark asked: "The hotel is still there? You have been there?"

All three of their hosts nodded in unison. Lise said: "We have happy memories of our time there before the war. We were only little, but one remembers things. We have been back there twice. No one there now has any knowledge of our grandparents."

"So — your grandparents — you know what happened to them?"

Mark expected one of the sisters to reply, but it was Helmut. "They died in a bombing raid on Dresden in 1940. He had business there we think, and they were visiting at the wrong time. It was a very savage raid." He smiled as he said it, obviously anxious not to appear bitter — as much as to say, the war is long gone and we are all friends now.

"Your mother is mentioned in these letters," said Mark. "Is she still alive?"

All three shook their heads. "No," said Lise. "She also was killed in an air raid and we were brought up by her sister — our Aunt of course. When it was evident as time went on, the war finished, and no news of our father, then it was assumed he had died. The command office in Berlin told mother that he was missing presumed dead, and that she should not expect him to return. They knew he was not a prisoner of war."

"And your great grandfather?" asked Sue. "There is mention of him in a letter here, and an interesting reference to an original *Der Rosenkavalier* manuscript, probably valuable, that he gave to your grandfather. Apparently the family had an estate in Celle. You know nothing of that?" They shook their heads. It was a thoughtful moment. The conversation lapsed.

Mark put his hand down into his briefcase again. "Something else that you should know about." He held up the other reply that they had received to the ad. "A law firm in Celle also wrote to us. With our small knowledge, we cannot see a connection with your father, but perhaps you will. " He passed the letter to Lise, who read it, and then shook her head, apparently mystified.

Helga reached for the folders with the original German documents in them and began to read through them thoroughly, passing them onto Lise. Mark took an initiative "We want to tell you that we know our work is mostly done. We felt from the moment of the discovery of your father that it should be our task to come and find you if we could, and bring you everything that we found. That we have done, but there is still the unsettled question of his remains. If we enquire into, and deal with, whatever regulations apply in your country and ours concerning his movement, would you like us to bring him back here?"

The two sisters looked at each other. Helga said: "We are extremely impressed with your kindness, and grateful for it. You have dealt with this whole matter very delicately. This is new to us. We did not know until you came what you may have to tell us. Are you staying here a little longer, or are you going straight back to England? Perhaps we should think about this all a little."

Sue said: "We are in no hurry. We can stay for several days if necessary, give you time to consider, and give any further help that we can." They arranged to meet again the next morning. Later in the day it would be impossible because of Helmut's work schedule, and he was the willing and necessary monitor of the conversations. He appeared with four wine glasses and a freshly opened bottle of hock. They toasted each other warmly, pleasure at a mission completed on one side, and ready gratitude on the other.

The overnight arrangement had allowed the sisters to find a sense of direction. When they met the next morning, Helga said: "Perhaps the most important thing for us to make a decision about is our father's remains. We like the idea of a funeral if it could be arranged — a simple service in a local church. We do not think he was a very religious man, but, even so, it would be proper to bid him farewell in a Christian way. After all, he is no longer lost. Then perhaps a cremation would be possible and we could bring the ashes back here. There is a military cemetery not far away where many men from the war are buried, and we think they would allow us to make that his final resting place.

Mark nodded. "Leave us to make some enquiries and suggest some arrangements. If you were to come to England, then we should expect you to do so as our guests."

Lise picked up the folder with her grandfather's last letter in it. "There are things mentioned here that are a surprise to us. You will realize that we were only young when the war started, and we only have confused memories of the preceding years. We have no memory of our great grandfather at all, and not much previous knowledge of him." She waved an arm round their lounge, and said with a smile "You can see that we are not prosperous. Comfortable and tidy perhaps, but not rich. Our mother apparently had no wealth or we would have known about it and benefited from it. She did her best for us while she could."

Mark asked: "Was nothing left to you by your father or his parents?"

"No. Not that we know of. We just grew up without any knowledge of them The aunt that brought us up knew vaguely about the *Friesinger Waldhaus* connection, but all she knew was what she had been told by our mother, and that — evidently — was not much. So much happened, and there were American soldiers using it for several years."

'It seems from this letter though, that your grandfather had a closet in the hotel that he used for storing valuable things. Your father evidently used to hide in it. You know nothing of that, of course?"

"No."

Sue said: "The closet was behind an access door to the brewery attached to the hotel. It could still be there. If it is, then the *Der Rosenkavalier* manuscript, and much else it seems, is still in it."

Helmut shook his head. "Yes, it is obviously valuable, and it could still be there, but legally it would belong to whoever owns the hotel now, would it not?"

"Legally, possibly, but morally, certainly not," said Sue very deliberately.

Mark said: "Do you have a computer — an internet connection?"

"No. We are not that modern I am afraid."

"May I use your 'phone?"

Helmut led him out to the kitchen where the house instrument was in a corner of a counter top. Mark rang John, finding him at home. "John. No lengthy explanations for the moment, but we are with the Bormanns in Halle. If you can spare a few minutes, please do a little internet search for me. It is likely to be a short one with a quick result, and perhaps you can ring me back here. There is going to be one — or perhaps more — websites devoted to the composer Richard Strauss. Somewhere memorabilia of his will be listed and preserved, in a dedicated museum perhaps, or in private collections. We are interested in that original copy of the manuscript of *Der Rosenkavalier* in the composer's own handwriting, so it will be a unique collector's item, and valuable. It's last certain location was in 1940 at the *Friesinger Waldhaus*, as you know. Is there any record of it being auctioned, or changing hands, or whatever. You may draw a blank in which case do not worry." The helpful John agreed and took down the return telephone number.

Back in the lounge, Mark explained the reason for the call. Helmut appeared with a coffee top-up. The sisters were more relaxed than they had been at the first meeting. They small-talked about their lives, Lise's son and his family in Cologne, Helga's home in Stuttgart, her husband, children and grandchildren. Mark and Sue told them about life in England, the university connections, and nursing in a town surgery. She also described the country home of Mark's mother, and the ridge of hillside with its copse, where Gunther had lain for all those years.

John called back. "Mark. It appears that there were several manuscripts in Strauss's own hand, generated by the need to edit and improve the work. Two of them are in the official collection. The location of the final copy is unknown, but it is on record as having belonged to a Kurt Feldman, who was a friend of Strauss's at the turn of the century. I am putting two and two together — as you will be — and seeing him as the grandfather mentioned in the Johann letter. Apparently he was a major shipbuilder in Hamburg at the time and had a large country estate near Cuxhavn. Strauss was a regular visitor and the records suggest that he worked on some of his compositions there."

Mark was surprised, but pleased. Some interesting history was emerging. He passed the information on, and, for the sisters, this was overwhelming news. Their great grandfather a major shipbuilder? There had been this sort of wealth in their family? He had known Richard Strauss? An estate at Cuxhavn? Another at Celle? And they had lived hard practical lives, unaware of any of it. It was apparent to Mark and Sue that this cascade of information was causing surprise and confusion. Helmut, who as translator had been the busiest of them, was just as bemused as Lise and Helga, his pleasant face a picture of puzzlement.

Sue said to Mark" 'Two things could have happened to that manuscript. It has either gone secretly into a private collection, or it is still in that closet in Munich. I suspect the latter. The grandparents, away in Dresden and dying there, would not have been able to liberate anything in their hotel — clothes, personal possessions, business records. Perhaps whoever took it over had no idea of the destiny of the Mullers, or of a hideaway, and Gunther was unable to use his knowledge of it. Shall we go and have a crafty ferret?"

"You are wicked, " said Mark, but with a broad smile. "We have time I suppose. If they agree of course." He said to them. "We have a suspicion that the Strauss papers are still hidden in the undiscovered cavity behind the paneling at the *Freisinger Waldhaus*. If they are, then rightfully they are yours, and they are valuable. We think that, if you agree, we might go down there and have a casual look. Would you like to come?"

Lise said: " But would not the people there now consider them to be rightfully theirs?"

"They could adopt that attitude if they themselves discovered the hiding place, " said Sue. "But it would be unjust if they were to get away with that claim legally. Not only that, but it also seems likely that the hotel would have become yours had the normal conditions of inheritance applied. The confusion of war and the deaths in your family interfered with things. Mark and I know very little about how yours laws work in Germany, but, in England certainly, you would be justified in researching the ownership history of the hotel and possible claiming it as a right. If your grandparents had not sold it or given it away with proper legal processes before they died, then it should have reverted to your deceased father, then to your mother, then to you. There were apparently no other lines of inheritance involved. You should know the truth about all this."

The sisters looked at each other in confusion and indecision — nervous and uncertain. Lise said: "This is a lot of trouble for you, but please go and see what you can find. We will wait to hear from you."

Helmut walked down the busy street with them. He said: "This has been a worry. They had to reply to your advertisement of course, but they had a great fear of what you might have to tell them and show them. They are both thoroughly honest, but they are not adventurous. Their early lives, like mine, were full of difficulty — all the violence and hardness of the war — and they are always reluctant to step outside the simple security that their hard lives have earned for them."

Standing by their car, Mark asked him: "Helmut, do you, or do they, think that we are interfering in your business by going to have a look at the hotel? We should not extend our involvement without your absolute approval."

Helmut said: "I know they are pleased to have your help and so am I. We trust you absolutely. After all, you could have kept all the letters to yourselves. Who would have known that they ever existed? Instead you have been kind enough to share your discoveries. We are very surprised, of course, and had no suspicion that the family had connections with a man like Strauss, and had estates. The fact that you are younger than us, and obviously very educated and worldly people, gives you an advantage when it comes to knowing what to do and how to do it. If we had learned these things from some other source, we would now be confused, and uncertain how to go on. Lise and Helga know that they must now consider whether they have missed out on an inheritance somehow, but for the moment they are pleased that you are here to point the way. We shall be very interested to know if you find out anything at the hotel."

It took them less than an hour to reach the *Friesinger Waldhaus*. The hotel was on the western fringe of Munich. It was an agglomeration of buildings, some obviously very old, with more recently added bedroom blocks. It occupied perhaps fifteen acres of sloping ground and was well cared for. It looked very busy as they approached, with the car park area well filled, but there were vacancies and they booked in for one night.

Mark and Sue had shared their thoughts on the way. There could be no question of discussing the possibility of an undiscovered hiding place with the hotel. As they had told the sisters, the moral right was on their side, and they had no intention of getting involved with legalities. They knew that if they asked about the closet they would be told nothing. Its discovery by the hotel, containing valuables, would be kept very quiet. It was to be a reconnoiter on behalf of the Lise and Helga. There was also the stark possibility that the closet no longer existed, having been discovered years ago.

After settling in, they explored a little. It was still daylight, so they could stroll the grounds. There was a public area of parkland through which guest traffic ran, and a separate driveway running up to the rear of what they identified as the kitchen. This was located in part of the original house, its windows fitted with air extractors. Leading from it was an enclosed walled area, and, beyond that at a lower level, a square building with high windows. The walls of this, Mark thought, were about sixty feet long. They were of ancient gray stone. The tiled roof had an open ventilator structure in its center. Two things were clear — it had been a brewery originally but no longer, and was now used as a storage area for the hotel. This then was their target.

To get a look down into the enclosed area, they went into the old building, and found their way to a first floor window that gave a view out on that side. This was at the end of a public corridor with function rooms leading off on both sides, so they did not feel furtive. They saw that there was a small courtyard below them with tables and chairs that was being used by the hotel staff as an open rest area. A shallow sloping ramp ran across this, apparently from the kitchen door to the old brewery. The entrance here had a large door that opened inwards and was held open. Through it they could see the start of a corridor. It was obviously a busy track. They thought that the old building would contain freezers and chilled storage, foodstuffs, probably bar stocks, and, in a separate area, janitorial supplies.

They went into the cocktail bar and considered what could be done. Sue said: "That is obviously where the secret closet is or was. Johann's letter to Gunther was specific about the location. If you are right and the building at the end of the yard is the old brewery, then that passage is where we must go. Question is — how? It is obviously a very busy track, people sitting about at tables during their breaks, and white-coated chefs charging up and down that ramp. It is not going to be easy"

Mark nodded. "I think our opportunity will come later. Bear in mind that this is dinner preparation time and it is an impressive menu. There will be a squad of busy people in there for much of the evening, but they do not work all night. At some point all they will be finished and they will go home. Perhaps one or two will stay to make sandwiches for late arrivals, and knock up coffees, but even that will finish. All the rooms have beverage facilities, and this bar has snacky stuff. My guess is that the kitchen will be cleaned and abandoned by

— maybe — eleven thirty. The bar closes at midnight. From then on the hotel will be in the hands of the night porter, who will be located in the reception area. The swing doors from the dining room into the kitchen, one pair in and one pair out in the usual way, will not be locked — they never are. And my guess is that the outside kitchen door is always unlocked. It is in an enclosed yard, and it is evidently a staff access, and some will have to be here very early in the morning."

'So you think we could go unnoticed through the kitchen after midnight?"

"Yes."

"How would you explain yourself if someone discovered you?"

"I saw a barman come in here earlier. I wonder if he is still here. I want to find out if the hotel has anything to help me sleep. I did not realize that this was the kitchen."

"Do you pass on this sort of wicked deviousness to your students?"

"All the time. It is central to my teaching program."

"If there was an undiscovered closet with things in it, they may amount to more than a handful. How would you get them out?"

"The walled area behind the kitchen has a door in it, with a staff car park at the back. That is the way most of them come and go obviously. I think it will be open. It will be dark, and I shall carry whatever I can straight round the lawn area to our car. If it needs two journeys, then I will make two journeys."

"Am I coming with you?"

"Probably best if you were to help in another way. We will be able to assess the chances and the risks as the evening finishes. Our presence in the bar or lounge will be innocent, and there will certainly be many other guests around. At the moment when we decide to do our worst, it would be appropriate for you to go and nobble the night porter, chat to him in your best German, or his probable good English, charm him with your best seductive smile, and ask him to point out some things on the Munich map that you would like to see. If you could keep him occupied for just five minutes, I should know by then whether we are on a wild goose chase or not. If not, then I shall already be on my way to the car with the goodies. Because we know almost exactly where to find the space behind the paneling, then all I have to do is remove some. I shall contrive that without difficulty."

"Leaving it undamaged?"

"A little perhaps, but not enough to worry anyone. They do not know there is a cavity there anyway, and it is all scruffy out there. Someone barged into it with a trolley, or fell against it with a sack of potatoes. Let's face it, the public areas here are immaculate, but that rear area is not so meticulously looked after."

They dined pleasantly and then went to claim a seat in the bar that had a view through to the kitchen doors. A cheerful blond was busy at the pumps, and they heard conversations around them in languages other than German, including some American accents. They were in a popular tourist area, dress tended to be informal, and the frothy German beers were popular.

As Mark had predicted, the staff traffic to the kitchen suddenly diminished once the last of the diners had risen from their tables. This was shortly after ten thirty. By eleven, the light level had been reduced, and there was no coming or going. The staff at the reception had been replaced by the night man, and guests in couples were beginning to make their way to the elevators. There was still a hum of chat around them, but it was getting quieter.

Mark nodded to Sue. "Let's go for it."

"Do be careful. It could be very embarrassing if it went wrong."

"They would hardly think I was trying to get into their safe. Kitchen areas are not a great temptation to the lawless. If there is a stache out there they will not know about it. I will play innocent — don't worry."

Sue wandered off nonchalantly in the direction of reception. Mark waited until the barmaid was facing away from the dining room area, and went through its arched entrance, leaving two unconsumed drinks, and his jacket on his chair. The world about him would assume that he had gone to find the restroom. Within seconds he was in the kitchen — cautious and watchful until he had assured himself that it was unoccupied. The door to the yard was shut, but unlocked. He closed it gently behind him. Still no one about. Ahead of him was the ramp and the corridor into the old brewery. He moved to the left and checked whether the access door to the car park was unlocked. It had been bolted. He withdrew the bolt and checked that it would open. It did.

There was no light in the yard. Going to the top of the ramp he could see down into the main storage area at the end of the sloping passage, where there was some distant illumination. In front of him the big old wooden door was held open with a wooden wedge driven beneath it. He kicked it out and allowed the door to close behind him. He had no torch, but could see that the walls were wooden, ancient, and deformed here and there. Rails had been installed in the passage at waist height, presumably to make the slope safer in winter when snow could find its way in here from the yard.

He knew that his target paneling was now immediately to his left, behind the door. The vertical planks of wood were about ten inches wide and no longer fitted together perfectly and they once may have. They were not tongue and grooved, so that he could see narrow slits of deep darkness between them. He pushed one experimentally. It moved, but obviously would not just fall out. Top and bottom were retaining slats. He needed a wrench of some sort. Back into the kitchen. Here he found a knife sharpener that would have proudly graced any butcher's shop in England. Within seconds he had edged the top slat away from the wall. He was able to lift one of the vertical boards straight out. He laid it on the floor quietly. Then his hands reached into the darkness of the cavity in the stone wall behind.

There was a wooden box — no, two wooden boxes, small chests, one on top of the other. He pulled them towards him,. Not enough clearance to get them out. Damn! He had to remove another board. The chests were weighty, but he knew he could manage both. He must. He put them on the floor beside him. Anything else in the darkness there? A quick search with reaching fingers. No — that was it. He reopened the big door, stopping to listen and watch before moving out. All quiet. Across the yard, putting the chests briefly onto the nearest of the staff tables. Open the outside door. Then across the deserted staff car park, through an open gate onto a veranda in front of the hotel that was busy during the day but now empty of people as he knew it would be. He moved away from the light that came from the lounge, walking across the grass more distantly. Their car was not far away. He took his time now. Casual walking, even with a heavy load clutched to his chest, would attract less attention than rushing. Soon the chests were safely locked into his car trunk.

He was not yet finished. The main objective had been achieved and he was jubilant, but he had to tidy up after him. It would not do to arouse suspicions. He returned the way he had come. He felt less vulnerable now because he was not carrying anything — just a wandering guest who had found himself in the wrong place. It was absolutely clear now that the hiding place had remained unknown and undiscovered, and therefore nothing would be missed. However, the cavity had to be closed. Cautiously back through the yard at the back of the kitchen, through the door, and within seconds the two planks were back in their original positions, and the slat pushed back. Not perfect, but it would do. He wedged the door open again. If it remained permanently open, as he thought it would be, then they would never know that the area behind it had been disturbed.

He had to return the knife sharpener. He bolted the yard door again and opened the outside kitchen door. All was quiet. He went to the swing doors, standing back from their windows at shoulder level, watching the distant barmaid to judge when the time would be right to re-emerge. The moment came and he was out, and moving casually back towards his chair. Sue was not there, so he strolled on into the reception area. She was standing with the night porter, deep in conversation, captivating him as she did everyone. Mark knew she had seen him, and would not have missed his ostentatious wink. He went back to his beer, giving her time to finish her task politely.

She was soon back with him, her hand reaching for his. "So?"

"So — good. I found it. There was some stuff in there, two small chests. It's all in the trunk of the car now — mission accomplished. They will never know."

"It was well hidden?"

"Not so much cleverly hidden as uninteresting — old wooden walls that have never been maintained properly. Nothing there that would tempt anyone to explore behind. I had to rip some wood away, but I was able to replace it reasonably tidily."

"So we now suppose that we have a precious piece of Strauss memorabilia in the trunk of our car — keeping company with two umbrellas and your unsavory tennis shoes."

He laughed. "Absolutely. Another drink?"

She raised her nose. "I do not normally associate with robbers and hoodlums, but, on this occasion..." They had two. They felt they had earned them.

6

Mark and Sue stood in the hotel car park next morning. They had enjoyed breakfast, but were preoccupied with a sense of personal impropriety. They felt somehow that they had taken advantage of the innocent. The fact that the little hiding place had remained undisturbed and undiscovered for over sixty years, and that its contents were about to be restored to their legitimate owners, softened their guilt, but they were still uncomfortable being here and were anxious to be gone. They had resisted the temptation to come out last night and examine the finds. It was dark, and there was no urgency.

Now they looked at the two chests, sitting in the trunk, with awe. They were obviously old. One was about two feet in length and a foot high. The other perhaps two-thirds its size. They were typical of mid-nineteenth century carpentry, a tropical hardwood — probably teak Mark thought — neatly dovetailed joints, brass hinges, hanging handles. They were in surprisingly good condition and the storage area had evidently been dry. The brass was tarnished to deep brown, but still obviously brass. Mark tried lifting the lid of the smaller one, but it was locked. So was the other. "No matter," said Sue. "Better if we stick to the rules of the game and do not examine the contents while we are on our own. At least they will know that they are the first to get a look, even if we have to break them open."

Mark nodded, and they began their return journey to Halle. He had already had a fragmented telephone conversation with Lise from their room, to tell her that the two boxes had been found. His German, although still primitive, had enabled him to tell her that they were on their way back. She told him that Helmut would be home for his afternoon break at three, but they would be welcome whenever they arrived.

They were still aware that they should not be interfering. They would be going home to arrange for Gunther's funeral. But their contribution to the unfolding of this family history had been completed. Perhaps there were precious items and information in these chests that would enable the sisters to improve their lifestyles. It had been clear to Mark and Sue from the start that they were far from rich, as they had said themselves.

Later, with the loquacious and agreeable Helmut keeping the chat flowing, they brought the chests into the little house. Within a short time they had discovered what two of the keys on Gunther's ring were for, and the locks were opened with a little help from some aerosol lubricant. Now the contents stared up at them, waiting for investigation. Mark and Sue were happy now to isolate themselves from the center of things. They sat quietly and watched while the family lifted the neatly assembled papers out gently, placing them in piles on their dining room table — exclaiming as they did so. Everything was in their language of course. The polite Helmut turned to their English guests occasionally to point out something interesting.

The *Rosenkavalier* was the target because they knew it would be there, but it did not instantly emerge. There were diaries, binders with sheets of meticulously-written small longhand, going back to 1902 — historic documents in their own right, but as yet of uncertain authorship. Much old correspondence, some of it apparently in the form of contracts and deeds, an old will in elaborate hand-written script made out in favor of a Frau Muller, newspaper cuttings and documents relating to the First World War, with mentions of Major Johann Muller. Folders of letters relating to the hotel business, documents that made it clear there were other hotels owned by the Mullers, receipts, and pages of accounts. A separate large envelope contained the title deeds of the Uhland Estate, near Celle.

In the smaller chest, papers were piled flat rather than vertically. Helmut removed a stack of them. Lise, standing by the table and looking down into the chest, uttered and exclamation, and went down on her knees to bring her closer. She produced a military Iron Cross, complete with its neck band, and a collection of photographs neatly bound with red ribbon, secured with bows. Beneath these again was a leather bag. She handed it up to Helmut. It had a draw-string fastening. Watched with bated breath by four sets of eyes, he undid the knot on top, and gently emptied the contents onto the table top. There was a gold pocket watch, obviously very old, a jeweled brooch with a matching necklace, and — wrapped separately in little packets of tissue paper, a mix of what were obviously valuable gemstones. The cut diamonds were unmistakable.

The Germans were now speechless, and they all sat. Then, after perhaps thirty seconds of bemused silence, Helmut went, as he always seemed to do at critical and emotional moments, to brew coffee. Mark and Sue remained quiet spectators, but they were just as caught up in the emotion. They felt pleasure at what was happening. It was clear that their intervention had righted a distant wrong. Helmut had been right to say, yesterday morning, that they could have ignored the documents found with Gunther's body, just leaving him as he was. A little more earth on top would have hidden him forever.

Over coffee, the sisters explored further, separating the chest contents into piles as they classified them. Then the correspondence with Strauss emerged, kept together in a separate folder. Helga took it and held it reverently. The prize was there. She lifted the front cover of the manuscript book, and saw the letter that had been placed there so many years before. She read it, watched again in expectation by everyone else. Reaching the last paragraph, she moved a hand to her throat with surprise, uttering an exclamation, and passed the whole folder to Lise, keeping it open. Lise also read it very deliberately, and then looked at her sister with raised eyebrows. So — now they knew. There had been an inheritance.

Lise passed the folder to Helmut to read, and then the conversation became animated and excited. Mark and Sue were totally lost, but not resentful. For the moment they were being ignored. Evidently there was something very interesting in that folder.

Helmut topped up the coffees, and brought them into things again, showing them the letter and translating it. "This is addressed to their grandfather, and was written in November 1938. It seems that their father had just been to see his grandfather — so, my wife's great grandfather — you understand? Yes — and he is about to leave Germany. This is so interesting. And there are two surprises here. One is that their great grandfather was evidently Jewish, which would have been a worry for him at that time — and he was rich. He had made arrangements for the family to benefit from his prosperity. This last paragraph says that he was to have an advertisement put in the papers in 1955 that his descendants could identify, and they could trace a source that would lead to the wealth he had left for them."

Sue said to Helmut: "Perhaps you could still arrange to claim whatever the legacy was?"

"Our only way would be to trace an advertisement published in 1955. That was a long time ago."

"The letter talks about German national newspapers. Which one do you see here? What do you read? Is it local or national?"

"We have the regional paper here, as you know because of your advertisement looking for us, and that is the *Bavarische Zeitung*. But I think it would count as national. People here do not read much else if they want a serious paper."

"Was it published back then do you think?"

"Certainly. It has always been there in my lifetime."

Mark said: " Well — they will have back copies going back to that time. They may not be the actual paper sheets, but they will have preserved all the contents, probably in the form of microfiche film. You could ask them."

Helmut nodded. This little piece of conversation had been between the three of them in English. He turned to the ladies, updated them, and then turned back to Mark. "Lise says that the diary is obviously that of her great grandfather, and they would need to examine it to learn about him. Obviously the advertisement would have been recognized by their father and mother, and their grandparents, but many of the things familiar to them would be lost to us now. We think that we should try to do some study before going through the paper."

He went on: "And there is another thing they want me to mention to you. The letter was written from an estate in Celle that this man left to his son, their grandfather. He says so just here. And here he mentions the name of the management company in Celle that ran things for him. It was left in their care. Perhaps they still exist and would have some information. Perhaps there is something here that could bring us great benefit. It may be that there is property that belongs to these ladies by right. It could make a lot of difference to us all."

Mark said: "Yes. There is much for you to think about." He hesitated, exchanging a glance with Sue. "We should leave you to your private thoughts. You would obviously like to go through these things in more detail, and — you are quite right — it would be a good thing to examine the diaries carefully. Everything is now personal to you, and I think we ought to leave you to it. We shall head off back to England in the morning. If you think we can be of more help, then you have our address and telephone number. As soon as we have some information for you about the funeral and cremation, we will be in touch."

They were surprised. Mark had intended, and thought he had succeeded, in telling them that he and Sue had no place here now. They appeared to think a little differently. Lise said: "We shall be sad about that. You have made all this possible, and you have helped to make sense of everything for us. Finding the chests was remarkable. We could never have done that. You are the sort of people who get things done." Helga said, with a smile: "A time will come when we will want to show you how grateful we are, and we shall look forward to seeing you again."

They nodded, hands were offered and shaken all round. Mark and Sue went back to their car. It was now late afternoon, so they headed west, intending to travel for two hours before looking for an overnight stop. Sue said: "I have a feeling that we are not done with this yet. They seem so dependent."

"Yes. But they have their extended family, the son in Cologne, and Helga's children, who are adult. Their thinking is going to be a little more modern. There will be computers there somewhere, and some twenty-first century awareness. If there had to be legal processes to reclaim property that rightfully should have come to them, then they will know how to get some good advice. And Helmut may not be a man with high social pretensions, but he is intelligent and practical."

"I wonder how much the stuff in the chests is worth? If the stones in that brooch and necklace are genuine, they will be very valuable The rubies in the center were as big as grapes, and all the other stones..."

"Likely to be genuine. Imitation stones are now easily made, but going back the technology didn't exist. They are obviously heirlooms. Perhaps the grandmother owned them as hand-me-downs."

"Sue went on: "And all the diamonds — beautifully cut — an eggcup full of them. Could be worth thousands."

"Let's hope so for their sake. And then there was dear old Strauss. I know that it is not unusual for old manuscripts like that to change hands in London auction houses for six figures of money."

"Well," said Sue, "At least they will owe us a nice dinner somewhere if they suddenly find themselves with full pockets."

Twenty-four hours later they were home, and mundane tasks faced them. Sue had the pleasure of another couple of days off. That evening they met John for a beer at their favorite pub, and updated him on what had been going on. The next day they went down to Mark's mother's, taking her out to lunch locally, and giving her an update also. She was pleased with the result of their efforts

The next day Mark and Sue went together to find their local vicar, enquiring about a funeral. They informed him confidentially, the first person outside the inner circle to be told, about the discovery of an aviator's body in mother's copse, their researches, and their visit to Germany to trace the relatives. Yes, a funeral would be easily arranged. He referred them to an undertaker who produced an instant quotation for them. The date remained to be fixed, but they could now pass on an idea of cost.

They now embarked on a period of routine quiet for almost a week, with Sue back at work, and Mark busy on garden projects, taking advantage of long days and the summer weather. Then Helmut rang in the middle of the afternoon. Mark was within earshot, shed his boots at the open French windows, and exchanged pleasantries with him.

The familiar voice said: "I think we need your help again Mark — in England this time."

"Tell me about it Helmut."

"Well — we did manage to get access to all the classified for sale advertisements in that edition of the paper, but it did take a long time to go through them. I could not help much, so it was down to the girls to read every one carefully It took them nearly two days, and the people in the newspaper office thought they were mad. However, they certainly did find it."

"Wonderful news then. They are pleased?"

"Of course."

"We hope it will be easy for you, but it may not. The advertisement gave a telephone number in London, but we know that the numbers are not written the same now as they were in 1955. If I give you the number, might you be able to check it out and find out who and where it was?"

Mark agreed and took the number down. His curiosity led him to another question. "Tell me Helmut — how was the advertisement worded.?"

It was in the for sale section as we knew it would be. I have it here. In English it would say 'for sale, three delightful holiday chalets, close to Cuxhavn on a nice beach, accommodating — Klara four — Rossa, two — and Lena, two. Call London owners,' and the prices are given. It is clever because Cuxhavn is not an attractive seaside area, and the prices asked are very high. So not many people would have bothered to reply, if any. Well, we know from our examination of the diaries, that the great grandfather had an estate at Cuxhavn, his yacht was called Klara, and Rossa and Lena were his two dogs that went everywhere with him."

"Is your wife pleased, and Helga?"

"Mark, they cannot believe what is happening. Neither can I. It is like a gift from Heaven. We have not been able to find out much yet about the value of the things in the chests, but Lise did take one of the smaller diamonds into a jewelers shop here in Halle this afternoon, and she was offered six thousand marks for it. We cannot trust them too much of course, so it may actually be worth twice that amount. The way things are going, we may just be able to have a holiday in a chalet on the Baltic this year — something we have never been able to afford!" His loud laughter down the 'phone caused Mark to remove it a little from his ear.

"You have somewhere safe to keep the valuable things?"

"We hope so. There is a branch of Helga's bank here, and she has arranged for us to have a safety deposit box there. We are not so bothered about most of the papers, but the Strauss is in there, and all the gems and jewelry."

"Helmut — give them both our love. Give me perhaps two days to enquire about that number and I will ring you back. I will call in the mid afternoon when I know you are at home."

Finding out about the number next day was not difficult. The local telephone people told him that they were often asked about old numbers. It was a Synagogue in West London. They gave him the up-to-date number. He and Sue had pondered a little. No one knew the destiny of the old great grandfather it seemed. They had seen his diaries, marveled at the tidy writing of the letter in front of the music manuscript, and tried to imagine the world in which this wealthy Jewish businessman had lived, with his business interests, and his estates in Cuxhavn and Celle. A man who loved dogs and was keen on yachting. And his son had evidently been reluctant to take over the Celle estate his son had bought for him just before the war. Perhaps not surprising in view of the tragic misfortune that befell the Jews before and during the war. So — where had this old man ended up?"

He rang Halle at three that afternoon. Helmut answered. Mark gave him the London number that would get him to the synagogue. "Do me a favor Helmut. We are very interested in what is happening.

When you get time, let us know how things work out. Who knows, you may have to come over here to follow things up. If you do, then we shall pick you up wherever you arrive, and you shall stay with us."

All was quiet for two days, and then there was another telephone call.

"Mr. Woodford?"

"Yes. In person."

"This is the West London Synagogue. I am Alec Jacobs, in the secretariat here. May I bother you a moment. We have had a puzzling telephone call from a man called Helmut Bormann in Halle, in Germany. He tells me that relatives of his by marriage, with the name Muller, were to call us in 1955 concerning bequests made by another German — Jewish certainly, which may account for our involvement — called Kurt Feldman. Our man was charming and very polite, but we are, for the moment, totally mystified. Such a long time ago. We had a few moments of conversation that led nowhere, and then he suggested that you would be able to clarify things a little. I am hoping that you can."

"Yes, I probably can Mr. Jacobs. The first thing I should assure you of is his honesty and the legitimacy of his enquiry. It stems from valid sources. I was with him in Halle just four days ago. Would it be possible to come and see you?"

"When Mr. Woodford?"

"When would be convenient Mr. Jacobs?"

"Tomorrow at ten?"

"Thanks. I shall be there. What address please?" Mark wrote it down and the short conversation ended.

So he thought, we remain involved. So be it.

7

The West London Synagogue was strikingly clean and well looked after. Clearly, it was not just a place of worship as a Christian Church would be. It was more of a community center, with an administration building that involved itself in wider Jewish interests and concerns. Mark was met by a receptionist who led him to Alec Jacob's office. He was perhaps a man of forty, dark, well-built, and formally dressed in a business suit, but there was nothing formal about his welcome. The offer of a brew — tea or coffee — what would you prefer? — preceded their chat. Some small talk soon established that they had things in common — Alec having been to Cambridge where he had read history. He knew the area where Mark lived.

"So, Mark. How did you get involved with a talkative German who is worried about an absent inheritance, and appears to think that I have it tucked in one of my desk drawers?"

Mark smiled. "It all started with the discovery of the body of a Second World War German pilot on our ground — a copse close to the family home. He had evidently fallen there from a damaged aircraft. It is an isolated spot. Over time his remains has subsided into the earth a little, but my wife and I gently dug him out and we were able to establish who he was from documents he carried. The placing of a small advertisement in a regional newspaper in Germany led to the tracing of his two daughters, one living in Halle, and one in Stuttgart. They are both in their sixties now of course."

Mark went on: "Well — we went over there a few days ago to return to them the things we had found on and around the skeleton, and to find out if they wanted him shipped back there for burial. It did not turn out to be the simple call we had expected. He was carrying letters on him from his parents that gave a hint of more in their history than they had ever known — the existence of a very wealthy Jewish great grandfather, and grandparents who, before the war at least, owned a group of hotels in the Munich area. What started as a mere courtesy from our point of view, developed into us helping these simple people to unravel some of their history."

"One of the things, evident from a written letter, was that the great grandfather — one Kurt Feldman — had decided during the thirties that it would not be safe for him to keep his wealth in Germany. He removed his money to safer places, with England as the principal focus apparently, creating a trust that would be administered here on his behalf. What has now come to light is that he instructed his son and grandson — our aviator — to watch for a press advertisement in Germany, appearing on a known date in 1955. Their familiarity with family affairs would enable them to identify the right one."

Well, the grandparents were killed in a bombing raid on Dresden, and our aviator died in 1940. Thus, the 1955 advertisement was not answered by anyone in the family. No one else other than those I have mentioned knew of it. But it did appear, and it gave your telephone number of the time as the contact. The fact is that this synagogue fits the formula of course. The question now is — what happened to that trust?"

Alec asked: "You yourself have seen these letters? You think that they represent the true situation? They are not some sort of wild goose chase?"

"We think not. We have certainties. A body, carrying letters, obviously authentic, appropriately dated and worded for the period — the finding of chests of family documents still hidden in an old hotel building from that time, and genuine evidence of family continuity from our Kurt Feldman down to the two sisters."

Alec sat back from his desk. "Well — whatever — this is all before my time of course. If what you are saying is true, and we did have some involvement with a trust, then your Kurt Feldman would have been known to us at that time. You say this was in the thirties?"

"So it seems."

"Where did he end up?"

"No one knows. Not yet anyway."

"If this had been a recent affair then I would have it all on computer, but certainly not that long ago. We have archives dating back to the turn of the century in our basement here, ordered on a year-by-year basis. Do you mind getting dusty?"

Alec led the way downstairs to an area below street level, turning on lights as he went. They entered a long room that was lined with metal shelving stacked tidily with cardboard boxes. He located and removed two from different parts of the system, and took them to a desk at the end. With the help of an angle-poise light, he looked at the indices on the box tops, running his finger down the entries methodically. He returned one box and came back with another, searching through the files within, and then opened one, leafing through its contents. Mark remained a silent and respectful spectator.

Alec turned to him and said. "You may be right about this. I have to look further, but I can confirm some of your suspicions. One of our community going back was a Kurt Feldman. He came from Hamburg in Germany in 1938 to settle here in London. We had apparently known him for some time previously because this index mentions earlier correspondence and two meetings with our administration at that time, both in 1935. He had what looks like a flat in Putney, in a nice area, and I have the address here, not that it would help you now to know it I suppose."

Mark remained silent, but hopeful now. "Ah," said Alec. "He died in 1942, at home apparently, and his funeral service was here." He looked at Mark. "Do you want me to copy any of these records?" Mark shook his head.

The search went on to find out if anything was known about a trust. "There are two directions in which to look," said Alec. "The time of the setting up, and the time of the settlement — if there was one. I can follow the lead back to the mid-thirties, but easier would be to see if anything happened in 1955. Bear with me a moment." Then: "No — nothing in 1955. Could it have been another year?"

"Please try 1956," said Mark. Yet another box appeared on the desk, and another search through an index. "Ah — eureka, this appears to be it," said Alec. He held up a file. "Let's go back up and see what we have found."

Back in his office he went slowly and methodically through the papers in the file. They were ring-bound in order. He put the file down and faced Mark across his desk. "There was a trust. It was set up progressively over three years, with the first contract in 1935. There is a long list of investments that your Mr. Feldman made here in Britain, mostly in property. The arrangement between us was that we would administer the trust on his behalf as a business, making a fair charge for so doing. He remained the legal owner of all the investments with us acting as his managing agents. There was an instruction from him, effective from 1935 at the outset, that an advertisement would be placed in eight named newspapers in 1955 — the wording here is in German. The respondents would have to prove in the usual way that they were descendants in the direct line. Apparently, only one person replied, a certain Gunther Muller, Kurt Feldman's grandson. He appears to have satisfied the trustees with his identity and entitlement, and the total estate was turned over to him in February 1957."

Mark clasped his hands to his head. "Theft — outrageous bloody theft!"

"What?" Alec was taken aback, shocked at the reaction.

"Gunther Muller was our dead aviator. The man we dug out of the copse. Someone was impersonating him. Oh man — there is skullduggery here!" He rose from his chair, moving across to look out of the office window at the busy street below.

"Are you telling me that we were deceived — that a person unknown presented themselves to us as the genuine claimant, an intentionally fraudulent act?"

"Yes — quite simply. That is the only explanation. As I was telling you earlier, only three people certainly knew of Kurt Feldman's intentions, his son and daughter-in-law, and the grandson. Oh yes — and it explains why there was a year's delay — no claim until 1956.

Whoever the villain was, he had found out that the ad. would appear in 1955. He reasoned that if it had not been responded to, and the transfer of the estate effected during that year, then the explanation would be that none of the entitled descendants had survived the war. He was right about that of course."

"But how would he know that the ad. had not been responded to?" asked a bemused Alec.

Mark resumed his seat. "If you, in the administration here at that time, and aware of the trust arrangements, had received a polite telephone call from Germany asking if anything had happened with a settlement yet, you would either have said yes sir – it was all dealt with last year, or no sir — we have been expecting a call, are you the claimant? Whichever — you told the villain all he needed to know."

Alec nodded, now apparently worried himself.

Mark said: "Let me reassure you about one thing Alec. I have no doubt that this office dealt with this matter with due caution and propriety. I simply think that your predecessors were taken in by a clever and well-planned deceit."

Thoughts were running through his mind, and inconsistencies emerging. "It would not have been a straightforward matter, let's face it. None of the genuinely entitled family were known to you — just distant names. The war was still a recent experience, and Germany was a confused and uncertain country. Had there been, as there obviously was not, a deluge of replies to the ad., then you would have had to impose some very thorough identity parameters. But, as it was, just one reply from a Muller who was able to present probably valid, or very valid-looking documentation to prove himself, and the matter was settled." He sank back into his chair again What to do now? He thought of the trio in Germany. What would they think of all this?

Alec said: "Well I must clearly, for all our sakes, research this thoroughly. Will you allow me some time to do that, and I will report to you on it? A couple of days perhaps."

"Of course. Tell me — is whoever dealt with this for you still about?"

"I don't know — because I don't know who dealt with it of course. But I can find out. It could be important?"

"Yes — perhaps — if only because he may remember the person or persons involved. Who knows, he may be able to identify a photograph or something — not that I have the faintest idea yet who the fraudster was."

Mark had one more question. "Tell me Alec. How much was the estate worth?"

Alec thought a moment, and then threw his arms wide. "Okay. Actually I should be cautious at this point because, strictly speaking, I should only part with that information with the authority with the owners thereof. However, in the circumstances, I think I can breach that rule. The estate's paper value in 1954 was just less than six million Sterling, after taxation and administration costs for that year."

"Thanks." Wow — a lot of money.

Driving home, Mark considered some of the possibilities. Several factors were important. Whoever had masqueraded as Gunther Muller had to be able to impersonate him. Age would have been important, and the general demeanor and manner of a cultured man. Whether or not he would have had to show that he had been a *Luftwaffe* pilot was uncertain. That stage of his life was somewhat ahead of the Feldman arrangement with London, but he would have had to produce authentic — or authentic-looking — documentation to prove his relationship with his grandfather — addresses, signatures. Would he have had to know that old Feldman died here in London in 1942? Probably not. How could he have found out with the war raging?

Certainties identified themselves in his mind. Someone had been able to access Feldman documentation and family records in sufficient detail and volume to carry off the deception. How would they have done that? Where would it have been? It was clear that Lise and Helga knew very little about their great grandfather. The chest recovered from the Munich hotel had some information in them about Feldman, including his diaries, but that would not have been sufficient to support a deceit.

The answer had to lie in Celle. The *Uhland* Estate. Feldman had bought it for his son and had written to inform him. Mark had seen that letter — Helmut's innocent translation. Johann, shortly to die in a Dresden air raid, never claimed it. Gunther was lying dead in a Buckinghamshire copse. What was happening at the estate in Celle now? If the old man abandoned it, expecting his son to arrive promptly and take it over, he may have left information there that pointed someone else towards fraud.

It suddenly occurred to him — of course — the second reply to their ad. The lawyer in Celle. What was that about? What possible reason could there be for someone there to ask about a long-dead Gunther Muller, mentioned in an ad. trying to locate his daughters? How had someone in Celle seen an advertisement placed in a Bavarian regional newspaper? This all needed looking into.

There was also the problem of Lise and Helga, and the agreeable Helmut. He had gone to the synagogue on their behalf. He had to share this information with them. Could the matter be put right? What would the German police do if asked? Time had passed and whoever had presented himself as Gunther in 1955 was either dead now or a very old man. His deception had succeeded. He had obtained all this vast wealth and had been able to do as he liked with it — passing it on to his family no doubt. Perhaps the family were innocent, having no knowledge of where their father had obtained his riches. What were they going to think if the police knocked on the door? That was — if the door could be found.

All these concerns had to be shared. There was a need to bounce this thing around with other people — other intelligences. Some clear thought was necessary. Some objectives had to be identified. He stopped his car in a lay-by and called Sue on his mobile. He told her the result of his synagogue visit. She was predictably shocked. Then John. Could they meet later? It was arranged.

Mark cracked open a bottle of wine in their garden later and the three of them sat, comfortable in the pleasant evening. The topic was less comfortable. John, once he had heard the news, said: "Of course you are right about Celle. That is where the trouble came from. If old Feldman had an estate there, then he had to have staff. If he was a moneyed man he had servants. If, as it seems, he was a man of affairs and had to travel somewhat, then he would often be away from his estate. It would have been administered in his absence by someone responsible — what we would call a bailiff in the old-fashioned way. Such a man could come and go as he pleased and be trusted to do so. Thus, if he had a wicked intentions, he would probably be able to access all the family records and create a persona for himself — biding his time if he had found out about the 1955 business."

"Let us assume that this person, whoever it was, did actually know of the arrangement to place an ad.in the paper, and the reason for it, then your analysis seems very likely Mark — all he had to do was wait until the year arrived, check on who else in the family had survived, and then step in once it became clear that none of them had. He would have known that there was a lot of money involved. It was worth the gamble."

"What gamble?" said Sue. "It was a safe thing to do. After all, had it not been for the discovery of Gunther, they would have got away with it forever."

They nodded. John said: "This other reply then — Celle. Are you thinking you may look into that?"

Mark said: "Their letter was on behalf of clients. Perhaps we can deduce that these clients are the descendants of the fraudster, and they remain aware that their inheritance was improperly obtained. Perhaps the appearance of an ad mentioning Gunther Muller alarmed them. Mention of the sisters would suggest to these villains that some of the family had survived, and knew, or were about to know, about their great grandfather and his affairs. Are they in the process of covering their backs now in case the whole thing blows up in their faces? Have they spent the last fifty years looking over their shoulders waiting for justice to pounce?"

Sue looked at Mark. "You are going to have to go back over there. This is the sort of thing that should be passed on to the Bormanns face to face. Then the decision will be up to them. Call the police, or what? And they have their wider family — their children. They should be involved. Theft or not — it is their problem."

John left them, asking to be kept informed. Mark rang Halle, avoiding making any mention of the synagogue meeting and its result. He told them he was coming over again and that there were other things to talk about. He was able to avoid getting into a complicated conversation because, fortunately, Helmut was working.

Sue and Mark talked long that evening. This was becoming a burden. Going again was obviously necessary, but would be expensive. Yes, they were comfortably off, both in settled professions, respected and valued for their abilities, but their income was not limitless. The novelty of Gunther and his affairs was wearing off. Sue was back at work again necessarily. Although Mark was not under pressure, he was beginning to resent the intrusion of this business on the other preoccupations of his life. This journey would be the last, and the Bormanns would have to use their own initiative. Mark booked a flight to Munich on line, and would hire a car there.

8

Mark arrived in Munich at one thirty next day. At least his familiarity with the town of Halle enabled him to drive straight to the area where he knew he could park. Then the short walk to the Bormann's.

Helga had gone home to Stuttgart. They had not thought that it would be necessary for her to remain here. Her own family affairs called her back and life went on. Helmut had arrived home from work a few minutes before Mark knocked on the door. They sat in the lounge again.

"We have a problem in England," said Mark. "The synagogue was very helpful, and they are looking into the whole business of the estate and the bequest. They were able to confirm to me while I was there that there had been a trust. However, the bad news is that someone — for the moment unknown — stepped in to claim it all in 1956, masquerading as Gunther Muller. There are no assets for you to claim." He expected them to be shocked, but they seemed not to be.

Helmut said: "We are not surprised in a way. It all seemed too good to be true. We could not imagine that something left in such a vague way would survive for over fifty years — such a long time. And, anyway, what was in the chests is turning out to be worth a lot of money, and it will change Lise and Helga's life somewhat. For that they are grateful to their grandfather. Perhaps we have gone as far as we can."

Mark shook his head. "I think not Helmut. You must understand that somebody deliberately robbed Lise and Helga of an inheritance that was left for them. Someone got to know of the circumstances and took advantage of them. Someone not too distant from Lise's great grandfather knew that he had left the country, that his son and daughter-in-law had not returned to their hotel after a visit to Dresden, and Lise's father had not returned from a raid on England in 1940. Whoever it was knew that the coast was clear for them to step in and claim the money. You cannot tell me now that you are going to ignore an obvious serious crime."

Lise said: "Perhaps it was not very much money anyway. Do we know?"

"Let me tell you that is was an immense amount of money then, and would be an immense amount of money now – close to six million English pounds in 1956. I have not worked it out, but it must be worth ten times that now."

They were both shocked. Lise said" "We had no idea that it could be that much."

"Just think of the benefit that it could bring to your children and Helga's, and their descendents. Look at it from another point of view — others somewhere living in comfort on money that is yours? You cannot permit that."

They both nodded.

"Should we talk to the police?" Helmut asked.

"Certainly not, " said Mark. "Not for the time being anyway. They would want to know where some of your information concerning Kurt Feldman and the bequest came from, and you would have to tell them that a bold interfering Englishman went on your behalf to break into a secret hiding place in a Munich hotel, coming away with two chests of documents and gemstones. Now — we know that, morally, right was on your side, and mine, but the police would have to take a different attitude. I could find myself behind bars somewhere, and so could you."

Mark went on: " It is obvious to us that whoever did this got their necessary information from Celle. It is evident that Johann Muller did not go up there immediately to claim the estate as the war was beginning, but there must have been somebody up there taking responsibility for it. That someone would have freedom to familiarize themselves with the Feldman background, going through the documents kept there probably. That person would then be well placed to go to London pretending to be Lise's father in 1956."

"We thought it was 1955."

"The explanation for the extra year is probably that these evil people wanted to be sure that no one else from the family would read the ad. and turn up to make a legitimate claim during 1955."

Lise asked: "So — what do you think we should do?"

"Have you told your children about this?"

"Yes," said Helmut, "they have all been informed."

"They must be anxious about getting a proper result."

"Certainly — they are all very excited, but that will change with your news."

Mark picked up his coffee cup, trying to think productively. As nice as these people were, he discounted getting much information from them. "We need to look at Celle. I shall go up there and see what I can find out. Do you have any objection to me doing that, or do you have any different ideas?"

They both shook their heads.

Back in the car, Mark headed north, having to deal with local rush-hour traffic as he left Halle, but making better progress during the mid evening. It was a long drive. He arrived at Celle at nine-thirty and booked into a roadside hotel. The first duty was to ring Sue. There was not much of an update to offer her, but they were close and the contact was precious. Tourist information leaflets in the reception area gave him an idea of the geography of the town. His first snoop in the morning would be the *Uhland* Estate. The clerk at the desk pointed it out for him on the town map.

He drove out to it after breakfast, finding it easily. The driveway had an old-fashioned entrance, with gatehouses either side, and iron gates secured open. There was a long drive through meadowland and ahead of him he could see a large house, probably built, he thought, around 1820. About twenty cars were parked on a paved forecourt. A discreet brass plate by the front steps identified the building as the head office of the Schiller Organization.

Boldness was the way ahead. He went up the steps into the hallway. Facing him was a desk with a lady receptionist. He said to her: "May I talk to you in English?" She nodded agreeably.

"I am not here for any business purpose. I have an interest in the history of this house. It was once the home of a Hamburg shipbuilder, a gentleman called Kurt Feldman. I know that he left here finally in 1938, but he was an interesting man and I am following up some of his life and times. I know, for instance, that his grandson, who was a pilot in the *Luftwaffe* during the war, came here to visit him not long before it started. Perhaps little of this is known now." He gave her an innocent and apologetic smile.

Her replying smile was also innocent. "Actually, we do have someone who shares your interest in the history of the house, but he is not here at the moment. Are you staying locally? I'm sure he would like to answer your questions, and perhaps show you round. Can he call you? May I have your name?"

"That would be good. Thank you." Mark took the fresh hotel receipt out of his hip pocket and showed it to her. She took down the telephone number. He said: "I shall be staying here for another couple of days probably, while I see what else I can find out about the family. This is where I shall be." He pointed at a small pile of colored brochures on her desk "These are about your business? May I take one?"

She nodded. As he went out of the car park she was on the step, and waved to him.

Back to the hotel, and he booked in again for tonight. He looked through the brochure. While conversational German was still a problem for him — a matter of speed — he found himself able now to understand sentences and phrases when he could meander through them in a leisurely way. The Schiller organization owned hotels throughout Europe, several chains, one of them a very familiar name in Britain. He found an index and ran his finger down it. Yes — there it was — the *Friesinger Waldhaus*, Munich. The plot was thickening. He drove back to Celle. Theories were becoming certainties suddenly.

The girl at the desk had been charming, but was she obeying orders from above — if anyone comes enquiring about things that may have happened in this house years ago, get their name and make sure we know where to find them. Why had she come out to the front of the big house as he left? To take his car number?

Was his theory right about the local lawyer who had replied to the ad. looking for the sisters — doing so on behalf of clients? Was the client the Schiller organization, or someone in the Schiller organization who knew about what may have been the source of its early funding, even if most of the current members of the board of directors did not? It seemed likely. It had been a risky thing to do. They must have thought about it carefully. Who is this putting an ad. in the paper looking for relatives of Kurt Feldman and Gunther Muller? Who are these relatives?

Shall we ignore it and pretend it means nothing to us, risking the possibility of someone arriving to tell us we have been involved in theft and false representation? Or shall we take the bull by the horns, replying to it and thereby pointing the finger at ourselves? At least in the latter case we would know who our enemy is turning out to be. We could check on them, talk to them, influence them, learn the extent of their knowledge and create protections against it. Advance warning would be valuable. Yes — reply to the ad. We need to know.

Mark walked the town of Celle, almost as a tourist would do, but he did not see much of it. His mind was full of what he now saw as a threat. He could not be certain yet. So far this whole affair had been a gentle process of investigation, starting with Muffin's curiosity, through to meeting the Bormanns, talking to Alec Jacobs in London, coming back to Halle, but now there was a sinister element appearing. There was a lot of money involved, and it had been dishonestly diverted. It seemed likely that the diversion had led to the establishment of a flourishing business. There was much at stake for those who had profited by it. It was highly unlikely that these people were going to say 'sorry, we were a bit naughty — here — you can have it all back.' Their attitude would be harder, covering their tracks, creating diversions, getting the best lawyers, adopting deceits, claming innocence.

He had a meal in the town and walked back to the hotel. There was a message waiting for him, ring a Herr Richter, and a number. Back in his room he dialed it.

"Herr Richter?"

"Ah, yes, Mr. Woodford. Good evening. Thank you for calling me back. You know I am a director at the Schiller Corporation. My area is mostly administration you know, but I had a message that you called at the house today, and you have an interest in its history? I have also been fascinated by the place since I first went there to work. I thought I would have a chat with you Have you been there before perhaps?"

" No. This was my first visit."

"You are from England of course."

"Yes — just having a look around." No sense, Mark thought, in beating about the bush. " I have recently come across some interesting history elsewhere, concerning the family of the man who owned the *Uhland* House in the 1930s, a shipbuilder called Kurt Feldman. I have some knowledge of his living descendents. He went to London just before the war started, getting away from the threat to the Jewish people of course. I expect you know all about that?"

"Well — yes, I have some knowledge. How interesting that you should meet some of his descendents, as you say. Are they in England, or here in Germany?"

"Well, they are spread about now rather, what with children and grandchildren. You know the way families expand..."

Herr Richter was persistent. "But perhaps the elder ones, grandchildren maybe, are still in Germany?"

Mark saw the danger suddenly. He kept his voice friendly and composed. "To be honest with you Herr Richter, I do not know, and I have not actually met any of them. My information is secondhand from a London source, but I believe they are still here in Germany, yes." He was fabricating now — suggesting innocence. "Perhaps you have met them?"

"No — I think not. Tell me Mr. Woodford, how is it that, after so many years, this interest in Kurt Feldman has emerged? Those of us who work in the house know about his Hamburg industrial connections, but we have always assumed that none of this descendents survived the war. Perhaps we should be pleased that they did. It would be interesting to be able to meet them. Welcome them back to the house for a visit perhaps? Do you know their names? Could we contact them direct?"

" I am sure they would be delighted to hear from you Herr Richter. I can try to get a message to them, suggesting that they call you."

"So you have a means to contact them of course."

"Well — I have a loose connection in London, this man I know, and they are known to him I believe."

The conversation ended there, just an exchange of thanks, and Mark was contemplating his performance. It was obvious now. Herr Richter had been fishing. Herr Richter knew that Mark Woodford knew he was fishing. Herr Richter had not believed a word Mark Woodford had said. Herr Richter would now be alarmed. He and his ilk had something to hide. Mark Woodford knew that they had something to hide, and he knew what it was. They knew he knew. They would have to take some action. There was too much at stake for them to ignore Mark's presence here and his curiosity.

He laid on his back on the bed, hands behind his head. This was becoming even more sinister. He had now talked to the enemy — chilling thought. He was miles away from the settled environment of his home, Sue, friends. And the Bormanns — they were in more danger than he was. If the *Uhland* House mob were the ruthless bunch he was now supposing them to be, they would act directly to protect themselves. If they were once able to identify the sources of danger to them, beyond Mark himself, then those sources of danger, Helmut and the sisters, were in danger themselves.

Would these people at *Uhland* House be capable of high crime? Clearly, with all the evidence now available to the Bormanns, followed up by the police, the Schiller group would be taken to the cleaners. It would be possible for a case to be made, starting in London at the synagogue, that would identify *Uhland* House as the starting point for the crime and deceit. The people there were obviously not the original fraudsters — they would now be six feet under, but there would be some who knew about the wickedness, and they would have to shut some mouths to be certain of safety. Hell — this was beginning to be very worrying.

Mark had intended to go home via Halle, giving the family some news about his visit here. He now thought that would be dangerous. He wondered about the phone on his bedside table. Would that be tapped? Anything was possible. Was he getting over cautious? Well — caution was prudent and you never knew. He went out to the car park and retrieved his mobile from the glove compartment. Then, back in his room, he called John in England.

"It's looking a bit black here John. I paid a brief visit to the Bormanns yesterday to tell them about the West London Synagogue, and now I am in Celle. I have made a visit to *Uhland* House. It is the headquarters of a large international hotel group, owning, amongst a long list of well-known hotels, the *Freisinger Waldhaus* would you believe. It is pretty certain now that they were the beneficiaries of the Feldman scam. After I had left there, I had a telephone call here at the hotel from a man who is one of their directors. He wanted to probe my knowledge, and the reason why I appeared at the house enquiring about Kurt Feldman. We had a conversation that dissatisfied us both — he not learning anything useful from me, and me knowing I was not deceiving him. It is now certain that they are warned about the danger of exposure. They do not know what or where the wider danger is, but they do know I know more than they could allow me to carry about with me — so I am getting out."

"Good heavens Mark — is it really that serious?"

"I have been asking myself that for the last hour John. Am I being alarmist? Am I panicking unnecessarily? Well, I am simply being realistic I hope. I have stick my head into the wasps' nest, and I think they may want to do something about that. Let me tell you more specifically why I want your help. The Bormanns should be made aware of this new serious angle to the whole affair. I do not think they are safe. I do not know whether the people here would have the means to trace them to Halle some way or another. Is anything known about them at the *Friesinger Waldhaus*, for instance? They have been there I know, and Lise Bormann told me that her parents were not remembered there. So, she must have asked them about it. Does someone local down there keep and eye on them in case they find out more than they should?"

"What can I do Mark?"

"Do what I cannot do as well as you John — call them and warn them. Tell them what I have said and what my fears are. Tell Lise to go and spend some time with her sister in Stuttgart. Tell Helmut to be careful about who he talks to."

"Okay. This is a good time to do it. I shall get straight onto it. Watch out for yourself meanwhile Mark."

"I intend to old chum." The mobile went into the zip-fronted pocket of his bag, and he began to assemble his belongings. There was a knock on the door. There was obviously no point in ignoring it. He went and opened it. A man stood there, thinnish, but tall, bespectacled, with a friendly face.

"Mr. Woodford." It was a statement, not a question.

"Yes."

"Gustav Richter." He held out his hand in an agreeable way that reminded Mark of students' parents who came to seek him occasionally at the college — respectful, almost self-deprecating. He shook the hand. There seemed to be no reason why he should not. "I thought I ought to come and talk to you a little more before you move on. Let me assure you that it is with the best intentions." He pointed over his shoulder. "There is a comfortable bar here. Can you spare a few minutes? Allow me to buy you a beer and we can sit quietly."

Mark was disarmed. This was civilized. There was going to be a sting in the tail, how could there not be, but for the moment, civilized. What point refusing? He nodded, and followed the German downstairs, through the reception area, and into the long bar, already humming with pre-dinner cocktailers.

The tables were low and the chairs comfortable. Gustav was

infectiously relaxed. He brought two beers across and laid back in his chair. His *'prost'* with a raised glass was warm. There was no hint of threat here. To all the world about them, they would appear as two friends stopping on the way home to lubricate themselves after a busy office day. Mark waited expectantly.

Gustav said: "I have a proposition for you Mark, and I shall come to that in a little while, but, for the moment perhaps, I should tell you very plainly why we at Schiller are worried about you, and the danger you represent to us. It is evident that you have innocently found out about a man called Kurt Feldman. It is very obvious that you have knowledge of him."

"We have known for some time that there had been some exposure somewhere. An advertisement appeared in the regional newspaper in Bavaria that referred to Kurt, and to the fact that, until early in the war, his son owned the *Freisinger Waldhaus* there. That was noticed by our manager at the hotel, and he sent it to us. We think that you, or someone known to you, placed that advertisement."

Mark remained silent. Gustav went on: "Let me now make an admission to you before we go any further. Kurt Feldman left an immense estate when he died. Predecessors of mine in our company, both now dead, knew that this was due to pass down to his descendents, and that an advertisement would be placed in German newspapers in 1955 to inform them of the method of claiming their inheritance. They also knew that no claim had been made at the end of that year, and assumed that they had not survived the war, a not unnatural assumption at that time. I am now going to admit to you that an improper act was committed — the careful preparation of a fraudulent application to the synagogue in London that was holding Feldman's estate in trust. There was a fortune in money and property involved, worth in the region of twelve million pounds. The application was made and duly accepted. That was illegal and dishonest, and I do not make any pretence to you that we suppose otherwise."

He went on calmly — a measured presentation. "This was many years ago, before your time or mine. That money was to become the cornerstone of our investment in the hotel business as a company. We had the estate here already, and the hotels in Munich which we took over when the son and his wife were killed in an air raid."

"How did you know about that?"

"I think I can admit to you that our information came from the man who ran the *Uhland* Estate for Feldman. He had access to all the necessary papers here. Feldman disappeared somewhere before the war started, expecting that his son would come and claim the estate, but he never did. Our man here was able to go to Munich in 1940. He learned of the deaths of the owners. He made what we would now regard as a spurious claim to ownership of the hotel. With his intimate knowledge of Feldman he was able to extend his existing authority, implying that the old man was still the source of his command. There was no one anywhere able to deny him. He offered the hotel to the military as a training establishment, and ran it for them throughout the war until the advancing Americans took it over. He retained it all when peace came. There were no other claimants — no dispute — and the same applied here."

"Let me come back to the ad. It surprised us for two reasons. One because it was all such a long time ago, and we in the company had begun to think that it could never be resurrected. Secondly, because it was evident that someone, somewhere, knew something about it obviously. It asked for two sisters, daughters of Johann Muller, late of *Friesinger Waldhaus*, to make contact. The existence of these sisters had always been known, but they were very small children during the war, brought up by an aunt, and detached from their family affairs."

"We have ignored them as a non risk. But, if these sisters were in fact living, then they would have a claim on us. Was the advertiser going to tell them about their right to claim — to tell them that they had been disadvantaged by a criminal act years ago? We have always assumed that the important facts were in our hands, and that no one else could point the finger at us."

"You will not be surprised if I tell you that we have always been worried about the criminal element in the original act. It was not proper then, and it would not be considered proper now. The perpetrator is dead, but it still remains a crime. It would not be difficult for the police to establish as a fact, that there are a few still — including me — within the Schiller group, who knew about the deceit, and we are therefore complicit in the crime."

Their glasses were now empty. Mark, without comment, picked both up and went to have them refilled. This was all very surprising — not the revelations, but the honesty. This man was making terrible admissions, and doing it with authority. What was it leading to? There was still danger here. He had admitted on the phone last night that the sisters lived, and were involved. Gunther? Could he admit to finding his remains as an explanation for the whole thing coming into the open? Probably yes. What was this man's proposition going to be?

He sat again. Gustav said: "Your ad. obviously brought a reply from the sisters. You admitted as much last night."

"Yes, but they knew nothing about the inheritance," lied Mark, "and they know nothing about it now. They are two elderly ladies, living very plain lives. They knew, from their childhood recollection, that their grandfather worked at the *Freisinger Waldhaus*, but they never knew that he owned it. They were only four and five years old when he died. Their mother, also a bombing raid victim apparently, never shared any information with them that was memorable or meaningful at their age. Kurt Feldman was Jewish, and, at that time particularly, it should not surprise us that people wanted to keep their distance from him and his affairs. Their father, Gunther, had been a *Luftwaffe* pilot, and all they knew of him was that he had been lost in action."

"Yes. We knew of him, but he was never found."

"He has been found now. I dug him up in England. It was letters he was carrying, still readable, that opened the door to all this."

Gustav nodded. "We wondered whether something like that had happened. And he was carrying information about the 1955 ad. in the papers?"

"Yes — as simple as that."

"And so it was your personal curiosity that led you to try and get more information about it?"

"Yes."

"I have to think that the sisters remain a threat to us of course."

"I cannot suppose that you will believe what I tell you. Let's face it, I did not convince you of my probity last night on the 'phone. But let me reassure about one thing — they know nothing that could be a danger to you. The reason for placing the ad. was simply to let them know that their father had been found in England, a moldering skeleton on a hillside owned by my mother. We simply thought that there could be living descendents. Documents found on their father's body supported that belief, and we thought they should know of his destiny. We are keeping his remains in England, and the sisters have asked for him to be cremated there. They know nothing of any information concerning Kurt Feldman that I have stumbled across."

"If you had achieved all that you intended simply by giving them information about their father, then you had already done that. So — why did you come here to have a nose about?"

Mark lied again: "Okay. I must admit to you that I did not give them all the letters their father was carrying. The one that gave information about the 1955 arrangement I kept to myself. It was clear to me as soon as I saw how they lived in Halle, that theirs was a modest working life. I could not see any point in raising any hopes for them about an inheritance that may have gone astray. But I did think that there had been some mischief, and all the fingers pointed to Celle as the source – including your reply to my ad."

"Your next step would have been the police?"

A very deliberate question Mark thought. He nodded slowly. "Probably. What other attitude would be appropriate?"

"You had no thought of enriching yourself personally?"

No — certainly not."

Well," said Gustav, leaning back in his chair again, "I rather wish you had answered yes to that question. I would be more comfortable at this moment if I recognized a little greed in you. What has to worry me about you is your honesty — your serious intentions. You are Mark Woodford, a lecturer in mathematics at Cambridge University. You have a settled appointment there and you are highly respected. You are the author of an academic work — 'The Conversion and Inversion of Formulae and their Simplification' that is read throughout the world by students. That amounts to respectability does it not?"

"You have been searching me out on the internet."

"Of course."

Gustav was thoughtful for a moment. Then he leaned forward. "Mark. Let me come to our proposition. I make it with the full approval of the senior directors of the Schiller Group. Not all of the directors now are aware of this scar in our history, but those of us who are have authority enough to apply measures to protect its secrecy. It would damage the company greatly if a scandal broke out, and we were to be brought before the law. We have more than two hundred hotels in the group, and employ nearly five thousand people. There is a lot at stake. I am authorized to give you now, as a gift, five hundred thousand pounds equivalent in Sterling, paid in Euros. That would be quickly transacted, a mere short drive to our bank and it is yours, either transmitted to you electronically, or you can have an account opened here. The condition for this payment is an absolute withdrawal by you from this affair. You would be required to keep any knowledge you have gained entirely to yourself, also ensuring that, if anyone else has knowledge that could compromise us, they remain silent also. By that I mean your wife, friends, whatever."

Mark was surprised. It showed. "Isn't that a dangerous thing to do? Have you no fear that I could reappear in ten years time and ask for more — wielding the threat of exposure again?"

"No. I do not like the idea of personal threats, but I am to tell you that if there was any suspicion that you were not keeping to your side of the bargain, then we would have to resort to more direct methods. I happen to be a peaceful and placid sort of person, but I have colleagues who are rather more ruthless. Let me tell you that there was a possibility last night that you would have been dealt with in a more conclusive way, if I can so describe it. But there were dangers in that obviously, not least of which were the doubts about how far you had spread your Feldman theories about. Removing you may have unleashed an uncontrollable hornets' nest of enquiry and accusation — official and unofficial."

"They have trusted me to deal with this in a peaceful way if possible, but I can tell you that extreme measures would be taken if you were to step out of line. And you must make sure that no one else steps out of line either. You and your family would be hunted down and removed. I think perhaps you would want to avoid that."

Mark pondered. Shocked and full of doubt. He wondered how he could deal with it honorably, and knew that there were few options. They were in a public place and he could walk out. Just refuse and find the nearest police station. Would he make it? *I have colleagues who are rather more ruthless.* Well — one thing was sure — half a million in the bank would be half a million the sisters could have, and should have – and keeping silent would be no problem.

Gustav's car was close to the door. Schiller, he told Mark, owned this hotel. Five minutes away was the bank, still open, and five minutes more made him the richer by half a million pounds. He just hoped that Sue would not check their balance before he had time to explain.

9

Mark had a restless night. What options had there been? Time spent with an apparently peaceful and quiet man chatting in a hotel bar, enjoying his beer, within feet of other drinkers, calm in this moment of conviviality. And then the sting in the tail offered in such a way that it was not refusable. There were no alternatives. How clever, and how unexpected — a bribe, accompanied with personal threat, to him and Sue, and whoever else incurred the wrath of the great Schiller organization. Involve the police? No — not sensible now. That would put Sue at risk. Gustav Richter had him by the short and curlies. He thought of dear Sue, now — at ten in the morning — busy with her hypochondriacs. Better not to worry her for the moment.

He had to go back to Halle, to neutralize as far as possible the dangers that lay there, and it was on the way back to Munich and home anyway. Hell! — what a mess to be in. What to do? Should he just abandon it all, giving the money to the Bormanns and offering them no explanations, no new dangerous information. Tell them to take it a shut up for ever. No! He could not leave it now. A serious crime, no matter how old, remained a serious crime, and now he had been drawn across the boundary of honesty to hover in the mist of wickedness. He had to find a way through it. Justice would have to be done in the end.

His mind buzzed with reconstruction, thinking through it all, and aware that the only proper thing to do now would be to involve the police — perhaps in England as a start. Taking the bribe had been defensive. Declaring its existence now to the police would not implicate him further. But, if he did, what then? Change his name, grow a beard, and remove him and Sue to a distant Australian outback settlement? Were he and his treasured wife to live the rest of their lives with a threat hovering over them? Clearly, there was no absolute way of controlling the possibility of a revelation from somewhere — the Bormanns giving someone a word out of place, the curiosity of their children, Helmut chatty at work, Jacobs in London forgetting himself. All very dangerous.

And another puzzle. Richter had said that the value of the trust recovered in London had been twelve million pounds. Alec Jacobs had said that it was worth something less than six million. Which of them had it wrong? Which had reason to deceive, or had been deceived? Both? Mark wondered about Jacobs at the West London synagogue. Had he not considered it necessary to give Mark the absolute truth? He was reluctant to talk about it anyway, and said so at the time. It remained confidential business between the synagogue and the beneficiaries of the estate, entitled or otherwise. But, in this case, why mention a figure at all? Jacobs could have said no. No information. Sorry. Mark would have accepted that, reluctantly or not. Had his apparent amiability been part of a clever deceit — thus far and no further?

He arrived in Halle just after midday. He wanted to talk to Helmut without the presence of the sisters. He went to the hotel where he worked and found him, busy amongst the tables, white-aproned and smart in the Bavarian fashion. They were to meet in the reception at two-thirty. Mark lunched elsewhere. Helmut was agreeable to a chat. No need to call Lise because his off times were unpredictable. A late sitting table could keep him busy beyond his normal finishing time.

They went to a bar that Helmut knew, just yards away, finding themselves a table and a beer. Mark, with some deliberate questions in his mind, said: "I wonder if you know a little more about what is going on than you have admitted so far."

Helmut looked at him in surprise. Clearly he had not expected such a direct and almost aggressive opening to this conversation. "What do you mean?"

"To start with, I mean that there are inconsistencies in some of the things you have said in my presence. Some comments that raise questions. These things were not necessarily obvious to me at the time you said them, but now I have had time to think I can see that they were odd. For instance, why was it that you gave the cause of the deaths of Lise and Helga's grandparents as a bombing raid on Dresden early in the war? There was no bombing on Dresden in 1940. I have checked. It was not adopted as a target until much later — almost at the end."

Helmut dropped his head, embarrassed. "It is a matter of memory I think — such a long time ago."

"And you asked Lise, in a surprised way, if her grandparents owned *Freisinger.* She had just said she knew little about them or their affairs. Did you ask the question because its possibility surprised you, almost as if you had connections with that place yourself at some previous time, and were aware of this family connection, but supposed that ownership was not involved?"

Helmut said nothing and was evasive in his manner — avoiding eye contact.

Mark went on ruthlessly. "And why was it that when I came back to visit you for the second time, you showed no surprise that the wealth had been claimed by someone else? You obviously have influence with Lise and Helga — you are a little more worldly perhaps. I think you had talked them out of any expectation because you know something they don't, and, as yet, I don't. You talked of the unlikelihood of anything being left there now for them to claim. Why? It's not logical. I expected the three of you to be waiting with bated breath for exciting news from me."

Mark intended that there should now be come clarifying revelations. He offered bait, in the form of an implied threat. It was a shot in the dark — win or lose. "My visit to Celle produced some fresh information Helmut — not all of it reflecting credit on those involved. I suggest you tell me what I want to know. And I have good reason now to believe that you know more than you have told me. What do you know of the family connection between Munich and Halle that we are for the moment unaware of?"

"*Verdamt.*" Helmut sagged — his voice becoming so quiet that is was difficult for Mark to hear it against the background of Tyrolean music and surrounding chatter.

"I am afraid to talk about it."

Well, thought Mark, that condemns you, an admission that you have something to talk about.

Helmut was still, and then he nodded slowly. "I will tell you. It is something I have been afraid of for many years. There were things happening back then. I have kept out of the way and kept the secret." He shrugged, and was silent for several seconds, turning then to face Mark, and taking a long draught from his stein.

"I went to work at the *Friesinger* in 1952. I was sixteen. They gave me a job as a waiter. It was being used then by the American army. It had become an untidy place. The German army had used it also, so it had not been a hotel in the normal way for many years — not like now. The man who owned it was a Herr Schwabl. He was not always there because he had other hotels, but we had a manager. I worked hard and when Schwabl came he used to take me off my usual normal work in the officers' mess as it was, and use me as a sort of personal assistant — fetching and carrying as you say."

"The first shock for me concerning Herr Schwabl was a conversation I had with another member of the staff there — Sebastian, the chef. He had been there since before the war and knew the original owners, the Mullers, very well. He had nice things to say about them always. Well, one afternoon I am sitting with him in the kitchen when all the work had been done, and he said to me that I would have liked the Mullers also. He asked me if I could keep a secret. What could I say to that? He told me that one night in 1943 when everyone in Germany was worrying about the war, and people's sons were being killed everywhere, and winning was not so certain, he was leaving *Friesinger* to go home locally on his bicycle. It was after midnight and very quiet."

"He was going down the drive at the back of the hotel when he heard voices somewhere — some shouting. He got off his bicycle and walked. He saw that the Muller's car had been stopped. They were returning from somewhere. No one knew Schwabl very well then, but he had visited several times and spent time with the Mullers. Everyone thought he was a friend of the colonel who ran the army training programme there then. He was standing by the car, leaning down to shout through the window. Well, Seb did not want to be seen, so he turned off down into the trees by the drive. Then he heard four shots. So, he made himself scarce. He said that the next morning Schwabl was at the hotel, but the Mullers were never seen again. He told everyone that they had gone north for a family visit and had been killed in an air raid in the Ruhr area. No one had reason to doubt him. He just took over, and was able to prove his authority to do so somehow. Seb was afraid to say anything of course. He told me he would have gone to work somewhere else, but in the war you could not just do that. He had to stay."

Mark shook his head in disbelief. He did not doubt the truth of the story, but he was shocked at the enormity of the crime. "And, of course, you came to believe, as your friend Seb must have done, that this was all to do with an ownership dispute, a local thing, partners falling out. You knew nothing about the other motives that we can now see — Schwabl clearing the way for a unobstructed claim on Kurt's wealth in 1955."

Helmut nodded. "Yes. And when you came to see us the first time, suddenly I could see the true explanation clearly."

"Have you not wondered that no one else hear the shots in the quiet of that night?"

Helmut shook his head deliberately. "No. There would have been guns everywhere at that time. The *Volkstrum*, the *Wehrmacht*, everywhere. And this was a training establishment, with men on firing ranges and working with explosives at odd hours. Bear in mind also that there was always a fear of the enemy arriving — parachutists. It had been happening. People did not hear all the news, just what the government wanted them to know, but if your son came home on leave then the real truths would come out, and spread. My father told me how shocked they were when they learned that Rommel had been driven out of Africa, but they did not get that from the official news."

Both men were thoughtful for a few moments. Mark went to fill up Helmut's glass again. Back in his chair he asked: "Do you know what happened to Gunther's wife, the sisters' mother?"

Helmut nodded slowly. "Yes. I think so. I stayed at *Friesinger*. Jobs were scarce after the war. Herr Schwabl renovated it all after the Americans left, and it became fashionable again. Well — in 1954 he called me into his office and I thought he was just going to give me some messaging work to do as usual, but he wanted to talk. He told me that he was transferring me to another hotel — the one where I work now. He had just bought it. He wanted me to come here, and he put me in charge of the dining room. Actually I was pleased because it would mean more money. It turned out to be not quite so simple as I had thought, because he told me he wanted me to trace two sisters here, whose mother had disappeared late in war as so many did."

"He told me their names were Lise and Helga Muller, and I was to find them and get to know how they lived. Had they moved away? What did they do? Who looked after them? I was to see if they had any memories of *Freisinger*. I was puzzled of course. I had never known them, but I put two and two together. They must be relatives of the original Mullers. He did not say why he wanted the information, but he did tell me to keep his interest quiet."

"Between my work periods I traced them. It did not take long. They had been brought up by their mother's sister. We were about the same age of course. We got to know each other. They told me that their mother Gisella had died in the war. Obeying my instructions, I explored their knowledge of *Freisinger*, and I was able to tell Schwabl when he came that they knew nothing, just distant childhood memories of being taken there, during the summers usually. They knew nothing of anyone there. They just thought of it as a place where their grandparents had worked before they were killed in the bombing. End of story."

"So," said Mark. "He was checking to see if they were likely to complete with him in 1955."

"Yes — I can see that now."

"And you married Lise."

"Yes, we took to each other. Schwabl rewarded me with two months wages as a bonus, and I was left here with an assurance that I would never be out of a job. I saw less of him as the company got bigger, but at least he kept that promise. A guarantee of work was precious in 1954 I can tell you."

"And you never told any of this to Lise, or Helga?"

"No. What would be the point. I had become fond of Lise. I have cared for her all these years. We have family. Those terrible times past have gone. I knew nothing, neither did they, about Kurt Feldman and his riches. And I was afraid about my knowledge — uncertain about it. I have often wondered what the *Polizei* would think about it now. Should I have told someone in authority what I had learned? Somehow I remained quiet about it all. I think it was for the best."

"Do you wonder, as I do, whether Schwabl also murdered Gisella?"

Helmut nodded. "But we shall never know." He spread his hands. "And I can tell you that there is another reason for being careful and not saying much. I think there is still some danger, mainly for the girls. You yourself would not be worrying about it all so much if there was not something serious to worry about."

Mark thought: "Is there no end to this business? It was clear now that Herr wicked Schwabl had paved the way for his excursion to London in 1956 with great thoroughness. Nothing had been left to chance, and there was still a Schwabl on the board of the Schiller organisation. Murders had a way of multiplying did they not — the first was difficult to do, but if others had to follow it became easier.

"The original Schwabl has gone now presumably — or else he is a very old man?"

"He died in Celle in 1978, about then, give or take a year."

"He had a son?"

"Yes. Max. He is a tough as his father. We see him occasionally. He makes time to talk to me. They must worry about me a little, but perhaps less as time goes on. One reason for my keeping quiet to you has been my fear that they would suspect me if they knew information had got out."

"You think he knows about his father's activities — the wickedness?"

"I have always supposed that he does, and I think now that — if the father did get money from London — then Max must know about it. He would have to be aware for the need for secrecy wouldn't he."

Mark sat back, thinking through what he had just learned. It explained much. It had not been a difficult interrogation. They were both on the same side in this affair after all. He wanted to put Helmut at ease now. Enough had been enough. At the forefront of his mind was the awareness of what a difficult place Germany would have been throughout the period following the war. There was hardship, recrimination, the superior and relentless attitude of the occupying forces, the presence then of a bullying Russia occupying the eastern part of the country, the personal humiliations, the ever present possibility that the country could become a battleground again. What chance had normality in this forbidding atmosphere, normal family values, normal honesty? It was to re-emerge, but only painfully.

He said: "Helmut. I want to thank you for putting me in the picture, and I want to reassure you that I do not condemn you for your past. During the time of your involvement with the older Schwabl you were young, innocent, and without any influence. At the age you were, you would have been accustomed to doing what you were told."

"Let me tell you that this conversation remains a secret between us. Not a word to Lise or Helga. However, I do need to tell you that at some time in the future it may become necessary for me to give this information to the police, but I am sure I could do so without involving you, and I would not do so anyway until any risk to you personally had been eliminated. If we have a priority, it is to return the wealth back to its rightful owners." He smiled at the cowed and uncertain head waiter.

Helmut nodded. Mark told him that he could see no need to visit the sisters for the present and that Helmut could keep this meeting to himself if he wished. However, he warned him to be certain not to talk to anyone beyond the inner circle, mentioning anything of what had happened. He explained to him that the Schiller people in Celle — his employers — who had responded to the ad. looking for the sisters, were aware that someone knew about the London trust. For the moment, all would remain peaceful, but if there were any disclosures, extreme unpleasantness could result. Helmut understood. They parted amicably.

Mark drove on to Munich, returned his car, and managed to get a seat on the next flight back to London. He was at home mid evening. Sue had been worried, as much by the absence of news as anything else. She had heard from John following his brief conversation with Mark in Celle, and had been aware that there had been difficulties.

Mark, who had nibbled on the flight, was in no mood to eat. They settled comfortably in their lounge, and the presence of a bottle of Liebfraumilch kept the Germanness in their lives.

Mark brought her up-to-date. She was astonished to learn of the half million now sitting tin their bank. She produced a letter addressed to him that had arrived that morning. She had read it. He did so. It was from Alec Jacobs, the amiable administrator at the West London Synagogue:

> Dear Mr. Woodford,
>
> Further to your visit, I have now had an opportunity to look into the records concerning the setting up of the trust administered by us on behalf of Kurt Feldman between 1935 and 1956. Inevitably, because of the time lapse, these records are not now as complete as we would have wished, it being standard practice here, conforming to normal office procedure, to discard files that are obsolete, or finally closed.
>
> However, we know that an approach was made to us in February 1956 by a Gunther Muller, presenting himself as the claimant to the estate. The

conditions of the setting up of the trust were such that he had to produce evidence of his identity, which he did in the normally accepted ways of driving license, employment documentation, proof of residential address, with the addition of photographic identification, and written confirmations from a legal practice, and one other professional person (in this case his physician). This man was able to satisfy the administrators here of his identity and probity on all counts.

The above conditions having been satisfactorily met in the judgment of the administrators, the assets of the estate, in the form of property titling and monies, valuations clarified by an up-to-date audit, were transferred to the said Gunther Muller in the form of deeds and a bank draft in March 1957. The matter was then considered closed.

Your concerns regarding false representation, mentioned to me at our meeting, are understood. However, I can confidently assure you that, as far as this office was concerned, the matter was dealt with in an acceptably regular and legal way, and that you would have to raise your doubts elsewhere if they continue to exist. We do have a duty to preserve the confidentiality of this transaction, and could only make further disclosures concerning it with the authority of Gunther Muller himself, or those who inherited his estate.

Yours sincerely, A Jacobs. Office Manager.

Mark re-read it. And again. "It's a bit savage isn't it? I suppose he has to handle it like this, and obviously he just cannot tell us everything. Mine was a casual enquiry after all, and I have no legal right to delve, have I."

Sue thought. "He is shrugging his shoulders rather at the

impersonation thing, almost as if it did not matter. I wonder if he has quietly mentioned it elsewhere — tried to get in touch with the family himself? You are now telling me that the fraudulent claimant was this Schwabl man from Celle — clearing out all the other possible and legitimate candidates for the wealth, and leaving himself with a clear field. One wonders what address he gave the West London Synagogue, the one they authenticated. And why does he not go a bit further, giving you authority to consult the police about it. After all, it was a crime, and although his administrators may — as he points out — have dealt with the matter honestly, you would think they would have an interest in resolving the matter legally. Why have they not gone to the police, who are above consideration of confidentiality anyway if they consider an investigation is justified in law?"

"Perhaps they have," said Mark. "Perhaps we could get a knock on the door at any time."

"Doubtful," said Sue. "He would have mentioned it. And another strange thing about the letter. He is not in total charge there is he? There is going to be a governing committee, comprising both the religious areas and administration. It will have a chairman — Alec's boss. Just think about it. You went to tell these people that, innocently or not, they were parties to a massive fraud. If it had been me hearing that I would have picked up the phone and called the head man immediately — 'Sir, I think you should know about this. I have just received some alarming information.' It seems from the letter that Alec dealt with this on his own authority. There is no mention of a consultation with his chiefs. Very odd."

"I bet there is more information in the synagogue basement than he is admitting to us."

"Bound to be. He is admitting that in his last paragraph, is he not. What might it tell us?"

"How much the settlement was for a start. We have a conflict of information on that now. There may be a signature or two. Documents. Addresses. As you have just said, this man had to tell them where to find him."

"Well — this Alec Jacobs is probably well within his rights limiting the information to what he told you here, and he is unlikely to expand on it. You, my dear man, can charm people a long way to get what you want, but even you have your limits." She became practical again. "Well, what now? Beam me up Scottie?"

Mark smiled. "I just think I may go and have a nose about in the basement of the synagogue."

"That would be utterly stupid. If you were caught you would get locked up. And, anyway, why have you become so hooked on all of this? Why put yourself at risk?"

"Sue, I am now, by definition, a criminal, and so also are you if we want to be blunt and realistic. We have half a million pounds in our bank account at this moment that does not belong to us. We are accumulating knowledge of terrible things that happened at the time of the Second World War, over-running into the fifties, and we are in some danger. There are ruthless people out there who would have a go at us if they thought we were not toeing their line. I have got to get us out of this, and the best way — as I see it — would be to find conclusive evidence against all the villains. If there was to be something informative in the synagogue records, something that they are reluctant to reveal, then I do not have to share that reluctance. Just suppose, for instance, that they are anxious to avoid bad publicity — 'synagogue involved in fortune fraud' headlines, and that sort of consideration rates higher in their priorities than revealing the truth. Also — whereas I can have a snoop in the basement there, the police would have to have court orders before they could do the same."

He went on: "I am not so worried about this as I was at the start. I have a valid and forceful story to tell to the police, and they will have to be brought into this before long. The amount of evidence we have now pointing to two murders, possibly three, and the evil of the original Schwabl, is compelling. However, the time is not right yet to spread the news to the law. Police everywhere act very deliberately and directly, and often not very delicately. Celle would know very quickly if an official investigation was put under way, and we would be at risk."

10

Mark went into London by train the next morning, open minded, but determined. He used the Underground to get close to the synagogue. He knew which was the window of Alec Jacob's office. Because it overlooked the central courtyard and faced inwards, it seemed safe to walk round the outside of the building, but as distantly as possible, to survey it unnoticed. The establishment was clearly divided into two sections — the temple area, a large hall with richly decorated windows, and the administration building, a separate structure linked to the other with a brick-built covered passageway.

He had to get into the basement, and he knew it could only be accessed from the central hallway, going downstairs. This was an old building and there were basement windows looking out onto narrow passages below, but adjacent to, the iron-railed pavements. He assumed that these windows would be locked, so there would be no way in there. There had been a receptionist in the hall on his first visit. When Alec Jacobs had escorted him down to the storage area, he had opened a drawer in the reception desk to remove a key that opened the door below. So, when the archive chamber was not in use, it was locked.

He thought that the office would work normal hours, but the spiritual side would have longer and more flexible working arrangements, with services in the evening perhaps, gatherings for instructional purposes, choir practices, weddings and funerals, whatever. Thus, there could be coming and going between the buildings unpredictably. However, it was unlikely that anyone would want to access the storage area out of office hours. It was probably the preserve of Alec Jacobs, and, if he was not there, it would be quiet.

Problem is, thought Mark, I cannot depend on this being a quick search. There were two possibilities. One — that there was nothing to be found, because it had been removed elsewhere or discarded, and — two — there was something there, but it was separately locked, or too well hidden for him to find. Either way, unlimited time would be precious, and that was only going to be available after the office had shut. How to get the key? Only possible if the lady at the reception desk was to abandon it for a while, and only during office hours. Unpredictable, and dangerous.

He withdrew to a distance, bought a paper, and sat on a park wall to keep watch. People came and went through the office entrance occasionally, up and down the stone steps to the street. At twelve thirty, the familiar figure of the receptionist he had met last week appeared, and walked purposefully off in the direction of the nearest main road. So — that was her off for a lunch break. No time for delicate and very deliberate decisions thought Mark, crossing the road through the traffic and making his way to the entrance steps. There was no one visible in the hallway, and the reception desk was unoccupied. Evidently, the girl abandoned it for an hour and there was no substitute — not an unusual arrangement in small business. There was a card by the desk phone inviting visitors to use it to announce their presence. The phone line would have been put through to someone upstairs, maybe Alec.

Quickly Mark had the drawer open and the flat brass key was in his pocket. Then he was gone again, through to the main road, moving briskly. He found a shoe repair shop within a short distance that had a key-cutting service. Within fifteen minutes he was back at the synagogue, boldly up the steps again. If there was anyone there now it would not matter. Alec? I am here to ask you another question or two. Someone else? Where is the nearest garage? There was no one there. Key returned. Mark listened intently, any sound from anywhere, footsteps? Voices? No. So, down to the basement, open the door, closing it gently behind him and locking it from the inside.

So far so good. Anyone wanting to check on the security here at the end of the day would find the key in the reception drawer, and the door secure. The priority now was to keep his head down. He explored the area and found four rooms interconnecting. The largest he was familiar with. There was good daylight coming through the windows. He found a quiet corner well away from the access door and resigned himself to wait. There could be no delving into the records until later, when all was quiet. He hoped not to have to hide himself if anyone came down here, skulking in the darkness.

He heard occasional movement in the reception area up the stairs, voices, often a one-sided telephone conversation, greetings, farewells, and the door to the street opening and closing. At five thirty he heard the door being locked. He waited for another half an hour and then went to work, for better or worse. Progressively he examined the boxes for 1955 and 1956, and then back, with a little more difficulty because they were in a different section, to 1935. There were separate folders and files for each month, recording accounting details, bank balances, contributions, private correspondence, the minutes of meetings, timetables for services, the come and go of a busy religious organization. All these records, spread across the years, reflected the advance of technology. The early boxes were heavy with red sealing wax, and much of the documentation hand-written. The occasional Hebrew was incomprehensible to Mark.

He was able to learn more of Kurt Feldman and the setting up of the trust. The file was very large and he limited himself to important details, ignoring the minutiae for the moment. He also found records relating to the final settlement and the payment in 1957. Puzzling discrepancies emerged and he realigned his searching several times to try and resolve them. It soon became evident that these were deliberate irregularities. It was getting dark now. He thought that he had found enough. He had justified the visit here. The synagogue itself was evidently blameless, but someone in its team had stepped out of line in a criminal way in 1955, and he now knew who it was. There could be no question of removing much in the way of documentation. It had to stay here, but he did fold several letters down to envelope size and put them in his inside jacket pocket.

He opened the access door carefully, locked it behind him, and climbed the stairs to the ground floor. It was almost totally dark in the reception. The only light was the yellow of street lamps shining into the windows on either side of the main entrance. The front door was locked and bolted, but this was not a self-locking system and he could not open it. Search for a key in the desk? No. That would require light and he was not going to risk exposure by switching one on. There had to be other ways out. He explored along the passage behind reception. There was a door at the end and he could see from an adjacent window that it opened into a passageway connecting with the worship area. There was no artificial light evident here, so Mark opened the door and went cautiously through. A quiet progress of perhaps forty feet brought him to an arch. He was now in the Synagogue's temple.

Because of the darkness, he assumed that there could not be anyone about, but he was wrong. Someone was there, sitting in a pew towards the back. They saw him. This was no time for panics, running for the door, dodging back out of sight into the passage again. He just walked slowly on towards the large doors at the back of the hall. As he was doing so, the figure in the pew rose, stepped back towards the door himself, and reached for the light switches. The whole area was then bathed in brightness.

The stranger was now between Mark and his exit. Both stood still and examined each other. One dark suited, middle-aged, bespectacled, wearing a skull cap, a look of puzzlement on his face. The other an uncowed, informally dressed, tousle-headed younger man, less than immaculate in appearance after his browsing through the dusty basement.

"Who are you?" Still surprised.

"Mark Woodford."

"Where did you come from? Who have you been with?" The manner of the questioning was not aggressive.

"I have been following up a meeting I had several days ago with Alec Jacobs, your administrator I think."

"But," spreading his arms to emphasize the question, "I saw him leave here at about five thirty. Has he come back? Is he in his office now?"

"No."

"Does he know you are here?"

" I hope not. And who are you may I ask?"

"I happen to be the Chief Rabbi here, but that is not important for the moment. What is important is that you appear to be trespassing. The passage you have just emerged from leads to our administration area. Access is strictly limited to members of our community or staff. How did you come to be there?"

Mark recognized that this threatened to be an insoluble dilemma. This man would be calling the police next. He would consider himself justified in doing so, and who could argue with the apparent reason? He softened his manner, from the confident to the more modest. "A former member of your staff, a predecessor of Alec Jacobs I imagine, committed an act of fraud in this building which enriched him by nearly six million pounds in 1957. I now have definite evidence that he did so. This is not a disclosure that I expected to make in this place, or at this time, but I acknowledge that you have a right to know why I am here, and that is the explanation." His final words echoed in this cavernous place.

The Rabbi was shocked, but disbelieving. The aura of respectability that came from the younger man, and his self-assurance, disarmed him a little. This was no prowling, furtive lout. He did not think in terms of personal danger. He moved to the nearest pew and sat. Mark remained standing. The Rabbi looked at him intently.

"Such a thing would be impossible — surely." The last word was added as a reassurance to himself. He wanted to know more.

Mark took his wallet from his hip pocket and removed one of his business cards, created for him as the standard form of introduction by the college. Its embossed crest was imposing. It impressed all were given it, and it impressed the Rabbi. He dropped his head for a moment, almost as if in prayer, which, Mark thought, he may have been. He saw no risk in unburdening himself to this man, clearly a pillar of this religious community. A connection between him and the wicked events of forty years ago was highly improbable.

"Is there somewhere where I could explain it all to you. I assure you that right and justice are on my side. Innocent people elsewhere have been seriously wronged by a criminal act, and I am unofficially looking into to it on their behalf. We are clearly in a place of quiet reverence here and you may have a better alternative."

The Rabbi nodded, rose, and led the way to the front of the hall. To the left, opposite the passage, was a smaller office area, obviously cleric's offices and robing rooms. Both sat, one each side of a tidy desk.

Mark said: "Please introduce yourself Rabbi."

"Hal Reznikov." His expression remained questioning. He was uncomfortable, looking at Mark enquiringly, now afraid of what he was about to hear because — whatever it was — it had a connection with this beloved place.

"I shall start from the beginning. In about 1930 a very rich German Jew called Kurt Feldman began to see, as did many others of your faith, that the future for Jews in the emerging Nazi Germany was going to be risky to say the least. He had made his money originally out of the meat business, and then out of building ships and operating them. When his gentile wife died at about that time, he decided to spread his assets more widely. His target was here, the United Kingdom. He bought property. In 1935 he came here, became known to this Jewish community, and arranged for a trust to be set up to manage his assets here, administered by you. This arrangement was legally established."

"In 1938, he decided to leave Germany, coming here to London. He died here in 1942. You handled his funeral. Before he came he had a meeting with his grandson — then a *Luftwaffe* pilot — to tell him that he, or his parents, Kurt's son and daughter-in-law, would be able to claim his assets by watching for an advertisement that would appear in the German national newspapers on a specified day in 1955. That ad. was duly published. It had been inserted by you in obedience to Feldman's instructions."

The Rabbi remained still, elbows on the desk, listening intently, straight-faced.

Mark went on: "A man replied to the ad. representing himself as the grandson, Gunther Muller. We have known all along that it could not be the genuine Gunther Muller, because his skeleton was dug up by me and my wife in a quiet spot in the Buckinghamshire countryside about five weeks ago. What I now know for certain as a result of raiding your old archives, is that a man called Heinrich Schwabl had arrived here saying he was Gunther Muller. This man had accessed family archives in Celle in Germany, and had worked for them as an estate administrator. He knew that the grandson had not survived the war, and he had murdered Kurt's son and his wife to make sure that they would not be able to claim the estate here either."

Hal spoke for the first time, raising a hand to demand an interruption. "You are saying that all those who may have had a claim on this estate had died or been murdered. So who are you acting for?"

"Kurt Feldman's two great granddaughters — now living in Halle and in their sixties. When we found their father's body and identified it, we also found letters that told us he had daughters. We put an advertisement in a paper in Germany and they replied."

Hal nodded.

Mark leaned forward, arms laid on the desk. They were now eye to eye, two honest minds. "I now know that this Schwabl man came here and made his case, but your administrator at that time, a man called Paul Jacobs apparently, saw through the deceit. There were elements in the identification procedure that did not match up. However, instead of sending the imposter on his way, your Paul Jacobs had another idea. He knew he had the authority here, and the trust of the directors, and he knew that he could get away with an audacious scheme — get this Schwabl to agree to halving the estate. He would process it through as if it were genuine and above board, and get half the money. That is what happened and I now have proof of it. Paul Jacobs engineered his personal enrichment to the tune of nearly six million pounds, a lot of money now, and immense wealth at that time."

Hal sat back. Now he was shocked, palms raised to either side of his chin. "You say you are certain of this now?"

"Quite certain. My certainty is not entirely as a result of what I have found in your archives, but what I have discovered dovetails in neatly with other known facts from elsewhere. It is probable that, had you, or someone here with authority, combed the records thoroughly, you would have remained in ignorance of the truth. Looking at them through my eyes, however, you would have spotted the incrimination. Mr. Paul Jacobs thought he had disguised his villainy. The law demands, then as now, that records of this sort be kept. So he spread them about in boxes, and he did it cleverly, but he would have been wiser to have thrown everything out."

"You know that he is Alec's father?"

"I did wonder."

"You know Alec, you say?"

" I had a meeting with him here last week. Talking to this synagogue about Kurt Feldman and his trust was the obvious thing for me to do. He was very agreeable — person to person — but what he was prepared to tell me was somewhat less than I needed to know. Hence my invasion of your privacy."

"Are we to suppose that Alec is in the know about the fraud?"

"Who knows. His father is dead?"

"No, I think he still lives."

"Here in London?"

"No. He went to Israel I think, and settled there. That was just after I had taken up my appointment here. I can remember how surprised everyone was."

"If he was as wealthy as we now suppose, it is not so surprising."

Hal nodded, his face now a picture of sadness and resignation.

Mark asked: "How is it that Alec had remained here? Does he have obvious wealth?"

"I do not know. He has done his work well, always reliable. We would have had no suspicion."

"Perhaps they thought, between them, that his remaining here in authority would be a protection against some later discovery. He would be the first to know after all. He almost succeeded in fending me off. If he had a share in the wealth, then I am sure he is enjoying it. It would have bought a nice house, comfort. Perhaps he lives in considerable luxury somewhere along the Thames Valley. His duties here are not arduous. A five-day week."

Hal rose, stood, hands in his pockets, head down, thoughtful. "Is all this easily proved? Could it be laid out on a desk logically so that we could see it clearly and understand it all?'"

"Yes Rabbi, but not yet. So much of the evidence is spread about, here and in Germany."

"You are asking me to take you on trust of course. Is there anyone I could ring now who would vouch for you and what you are telling me — someone responsible?" He looked directly at Mark.

"I can give you the number of a Cambridge University Professor of Chemistry, Dr. John Shaw, who apart from his other talents, speaks fluent German. He translated the documents we found on the body, and remains privy to all that I am doing." He reached for his wallet again.

Hal raised a hand. "No — don't bother. What are you going to do with all this information?"

"Give it to the Feldman descendents, the sisters in Halle. It is their business. They may want to talk to the German police about it I suppose, now that fraud is clearly evident."

"So we shall be hearing from them, via the London police I imagine"

"I expect so. Some involvement for you is inevitable, but you obviously have nothing to fear personally. There can be a bad apple in any good barrel after all. What I can now see is that a police investigation is going to be complex, not only because we now have three big countries involved, with separate and differing legal and judicial systems, but because it took seventy years for the whole story to unfold, and most of the miscreants are dead."

"Probably just as well," said the Rabbi feelingly.

They walked back out towards the front doors, Mark said: "I

should tell you that I am sorry to have interrupted your quiet contemplations so abruptly, and with such unwelcome news. You know where to find me if you need to. I am glad to have met you."

I wish I could say the same for you," said the Rabbi dryly. But he held out a firm hand to be shaken as they said goodbye on the pavement.

11

When Paul Jacobs and Heinrich Schwabl connived to convert someone else's inheritance into their own joint profit in 1956, they were an odd couple. Theirs was a marriage of convenience — not taste. On one side was a quiet Jew who had been swayed away from a life of modest rectitude by the temptations of considerable wealth, and on the other side was a Nazi who bitterly resented the failure of his country to follow up its promise of supremacy for the Arian.

Mutual distrust became a security between them. Each knew that the other could, if he so chose, blow the other away with a disclosure to the legal authorities, having prepared the way for their own escape to safety before doing so. They came to an agreement. Most of the wealth was in property, not cash. There were substantial rentals, so that there was no shortage of ongoing income, but their joint objective was clear — sell the property. They sensibly agreed that there could be no urgency about this. It should be done progressively, watching for the emergence of favorable market conditions, responding to demand. They believed that they had covered their tracks well, and there was scant chance of their wrongdoing coming dangerously to light. Paul had the trust of the synagogue and the affair was closed as far as they were concerned. Max assured him that there were no claimants left in Germany.

Most of the property was sold within two years, but some simply would not sell. A valuable warehouse in east London stood in an area where redevelopment was expected. Decisions had not been finalized by the local authority, so no one would buy it while there was doubt about its destiny. There were other sites where similar uncertainties became a deterrent to sale. Thus, there had to be a continuing collaboration. It was not a case of thanks and goodbye.

Paul was twenty-eight. Not yet married. Subject to the need to have occasional contact with Heinrich, he was free now to do as he liked. He carried on as administrator at the West London Synagogue, the simple reason for doing so being his personal security. The assurances of Heinrich that there would be no claimants from Germany did not entirely convince him. The fact that the advertisement in the German papers had produced only one reply was encouraging, but there was a lurking uncertainty. Heinrich's noisy Teutonic confidence — you can trust me, all will be well — did not reassure him absolutely. He thought it prudent to remain in post for the time being, master of his records, and first to know if there was to be a threat of embarrassing disclosure.

By 1960 he thought that the likelihood of trouble had evaporated. Three clear years had passed. He advanced his life plan to stage two, emigrating to Israel. Other Jews were doing this, most of them coming from troubled areas of the world, including North Africa at this time, and their reasons were to find hope and security. Most of them arrived in poverty. For Paul, however, with his wealth, it was to prove a move into comfort, with a motive. He would, at any time he chose, release himself from the troubles and insecurities of the troubled narrow strip of desert in the eastern Mediterranean, and go to the comfort of America. He would, in the meantime, allow himself to be reabsorbed into total Jewishness, becoming a citizen, keeping his nose clean, and using alternative identities occasionally. He knew that this small country was grateful for the arrival of anyone of their faith who could be self-supporting, and who extended good will to the nation by giving their time to its institutions, in his case by offering his accounting skills gratis to several kibbutzim.

He lived in modest temporary comfort. To his neighbors, in one of Haifa's more comfortable apartment blocks, he appeared to be self-denying and devout, but there was wine if he fancied it, and plenty of taxis in the busy street below to take him wherever he wanted. He kept his head down, obeyed all the social rules, and could disappear to have the best dinner in town if the mood took him. Money buys everything.

He met and married a nice young lady, giving her a fabricated explanation for his wealth, most of which was now safely in the United States. They produced a son and called him Alec. In 1968 they made a visit to England, renewed acquaintance with friends and former colleagues at the synagogue, and made arrangements for Alec to be educated at a private school in Berkshire. He duly arrived there.

In 1972 they migrated to America, having paved the way with a couple of visits to buy a comfortable property in West Virginia. America, like Israel, always welcomes those who are able to look after themselves. They became absorbed into the local Jewish community. Eventually the bright Alec earned his way into Cambridge University where he did well. He had become accustomed to living a life of separation from his parents, but resented it less than he might otherwise have done because they always made sure he was well funded, and came over to visit him regularly.

The time came when Paul needed to tell him certain things. He explained the source of his wealth to him almost honestly. He softened his guilt, if there was any remaining, by telling Alec that an inheritance had been left in London for a German family, but they had all died in the war. Paul had been its custodian. Its growth, he said, had depended on him. Left unclaimed, the estate would just have lain there, accumulating value, and with no one benefiting. An amiable German had eventually appeared and claimed it, and he was able to reassure Paul that none of the entitled family remained, and that it would be a shame to allow it all to go to waste indefinitely. Paul had agreed. He thought that those who had a right to it are unable to enjoy it, so we may as well. He made it sound almost respectable.

He told Alec that he wanted him to work at the West London Synagogue. He knew that there was information on file there that could point an accusing finger at him if it was cleverly assembled. At the time it was generated it had to be kept. The advances of the computer age worried him particularly — what if all the old papers were processed into a modern system. That could be dangerous, and he could not just wander in and alter any of the records now.

He encouraged Alec. He would, anyway, be the sole inheritor of the Jacob's wealth eventually, and, meanwhile, Paul would transfer funds to him regularly to enable him to marry if he wished and live a comfortable life. If he wanted to pursue some more intellectual avenues — authorship, study, whatever, then he would have time to dedicate to these things because, after all, his office hours would be short. With that assurance Alec agreed. On his next visit to London, Paul made the necessary arrangements. His good reputation there helped. Alec joined as an assistant in 1990, and became manager of the office two years later.

Heinrich Schwabl had no reluctances or reservations. He had been the prime mover in the fraud plan, reluctantly accepting Paul Jacobs as an inevitable and unavoidable accomplice. No matter — six million was still a lot of money. He had already taken possession, indisputably legal in the absence of any dissent, of the Celle estate, and the six hotels in the *Freisinger* group. He was already wealthy in 1957. He had been married for eight years by then anyway, and had a young family. He had great expectations of his eldest son, who was eventually brought into the growing business, and quickly established himself as a quick thinking and bright executive.

The Schwabls, father and son, shared a common attitude to the world. It does what we require of it, and, if it does not, then we straighten it out in such a way that it does. If Paul Jacobs revelations to his son had been overlaid with some embarrassment, Heinrich's necessary sharing of information with Max was less so. There was no place for modesty or conscience here. He wanted the hotels, The *Uhland* estate, and *Friesinger*, and was going to have them. He wanted to be able to claim the Feldman inheritance in London successfully, and he regarded his half share as satisfactory in the circumstances. Some unimportant people had been killed along the way. So what? At the time people were dying all over the place and, let's face it, this is Jewish money. Better that we should have it than some scruffy descendents somewhere. We are making good use of it.

When his father died, Max took over control. The Schiller Group had become a public company, but he kept a majority holding. They traded successfully, so their stock valuations were always high. Of the members of the board of directors, only four knew of the Feldman connection and its valuable contribution to their early years of business. One of them was Gustav Richter. He and Max worked closely together, each aware of, and respecting, their contrasting talents — Max the do it my way toughie, and Gustav the let's chat about it smoothie. They were sitting together in Max's office in Celle, two days after Mark had invaded the London Synagogue. It was Saturday, mid-morning.

Max, broad shouldered, russet-haired and ruddy, had his shirt sleeves rolled up, and the knot of his tie was at half mast, his top shirt button opened. "Well. Who is this bastard Englishman anyway?"

"He is a lecturer in mathematics at Cambridge University in England, married, quite ordinary really. Agreeable sort of chap. Intelligent. Courteous."

"And he dug Gunther Muller out of his garden?"

"His mother's"

"And, as we agreed — your recommendation — we have given him the equivalent of half a million in Sterling."

"Yes."

"And that was on condition that this intelligent scholar go away and forget about anything he had discovered concerning the Feldman business in London."

"Yes."

"And then I get an anxious telephone call at home last night from Jacobs in America telling me his son had been nobbled by his bosses at the Synagogue in London. They said that a man had come to see them questioning the validity of the transfer of the estate of Feldman to his family in 1956. They asked for the son to get information out of their archives, enabling them to examine it. If his fear is right, and we are on the point of some sort of dangerous exposure resulting from the interference of your mathematical swine, do you still think that your way of handling this is working?"

"I still think that money is a better way of persuading that the threat of violence is — yes. Anyway, what happened in London?"

"It's a bit unclear for the moment, because the son, Alec Jacobs, has made himself scarce at this father's request. He may be on his way to America. Apparently he was called in by one of the Rabbis that he works for. So, someone somewhere has a finger pointing at us, and there can only be one reason why. It is a knock on from that damned advertisement — looking for two daughters in Bavaria."

"Yes Max, that is a possibility, but bear in mind that our man Woodford had already put the word about here and there. Other people are in the know. He talked about a man in London. The daughters have been traced. It could be that he is trying to close the doors to comply with us for his own protection. I told him that our condition was that he shut up himself and shut everyone else up. It may take him a day or two to get round them and quieten them down. Perhaps whatever has alarmed the synagogue in London was as a result of something he had set in motion before I met him. I know he had been there asking about the estate because he told me so."

Max stood up and turned, hands in pockets, looking out of the first floor window behind his desk. "Did you tell this man in no uncertain terms that if he stepped out of line, we would have other ways of making him keep silent?"

"Yes — I made that clear." Gustav was talking to his boss's back. "There was no mention of police?"

"No, not in London. Not yet anyway."

"One consolation is that Alec Jacobs would be the first target if there was a problem. It was he that put his fingers in the till. If the son is on his way to America then the first focus of interest would be over there."

"I would take more comfort from that, Gustav, had it not been for your Englishman coming here to have a nose about." He was thoughtful for a moment. "The question now is, what evidence do they have pointing at us? That has to be our worry. My father effectively cleared his route when he went over there. There was nothing in writing involving him. We knew that the two sisters in Halle knew nothing. The Jew in London that had the half share must have covered his tracks, and so he must have covered father's — they were in it together. And this Englishman? What could he have found out?"

"Obviously, there must have been some information on the body of Gunther Muller when they dug him up. Only that would explain them advertising to find relatives in an innocent way."

"That is clear. He had documentation on him that gave his name and address, and perhaps some additional information that led them to believe there were daughters — a letter from his wife or something. But how did they find out about Feldman?"

"We have always regarded the sisters as simple and harmless people, but supposing this Englishman began to research their background a bit. Would they have remembered *Friesinger*? Probably. Is there anyone there now who could have pointed him in our direction, remembering Feldman and your father's interest down there when the war was on?"

"Doubtful. It is a completely different staff, top to bottom. Tell me then Gustav — where do you think the principal threat to us is now? Even if I go along with your theory that this Englishman is covering his tracks in an effort to comply with your demands, it is evident that there is still some information out there that is dangerous. Where is it?"

"The main danger as I see it, is the synagogue in London. The transfer of the estate took place within the framework of the law in Britain. They must have kept records. Wasn't it a matter of cautious security that led Jacobs to make his son get a job there, and keep a look out for trouble if it came – fears related to the advance of computerization?"

"Well then. Should we organize a pounce on the synagogue? Clear out their records. If that is where the danger is, there would be no danger with them disposed of."

"It would have to be carefully handled," said Gustav. "The English police would be involved straight away. The encouraging element for us is that the people over there are evidently puzzled rather then certain. If we could get everything out then there would be no way they could resolve the puzzle."

"Hell! One thing is certain — we have to act quickly. If necessary, this Englishman will have to go. This is a situation that could quickly get out of hand."

"The danger is that we do not know how many others have been briefed by Woodford. His wife, friends? If we were to take the 'wipe them out' route, we would have to go for the lot or nothing. It would be pointless to remove him, only to find someone emerging from behind him ready to blow the whistle. That is why I thought a bribe was the best way forward."

"You may be right. We shall see, and I am prepared to let it rest there for the moment as far as he is concerned. However, the synagogue has to be dealt with — now. We remove the threat very deliberately. Fire probably — the best way if there is a lot of paper involved. Will you get them onto it?"

"Yes. Right away."

Five hundred miles away, Mark was, at the same moment, at home when the 'phone rang. It was the Rabbi, Hal Reznikov. "Mr. Woodford?"

"Good morning Rabbi."

"I just wanted to have a short talk with you if I may. It was rather a shock meeting you two nights ago. You will gather that I was surprised to encounter you."

"Of course."

"You have presented us with something of a quandary. I have no doubt that your concerns are validly based, but we have a problem for the moment accessing our files. The only man who understands the system thoroughly, Alec Jacobs, is unavailable for the moment. We have things in the basement that go back many years as you know."

"Yes."

"We shall be having a management meeting at the house of one of our elders locally this evening, and I would like to give them something rather more in the way of an informed briefing than I am able to do at the moment. When we talked, I heard much, but remembered little. It was all so confusing with the surprise element. May I just ask you one or two things that may help us?"

Mark saw his dilemma. "Rabbi. I have been well aware that our encounter must have raised more questions than it provided answers, and you have now, whether you like it or not, been plunged into the middle of things. I am going to suggest that I come down and give you, and anyone else involved, a detailed briefing, and perhaps I can meet you first so that we can assemble some documents, and I can give you a preview. Apart from anything else, I have copies here of everything that was found on Gunther Muller when we unearthed him, and that is where our first clue to possible improper goings on emerged. If you are meeting this evening, are you free at the synagogue this afternoon?"

"That is very good of you. Yes, I can arrange to be here from lunchtime onwards."

"Do you have a lawyer?"

"We know the importance of that. He will be present this evening."

12

For Sue, the unfolding of this affair had been uncomfortable. She had a job to do and had to be there. Thus she was necessarily detached from what had been going on — anxious for Mark and eager to contribute, but unable to do much other than give encouragement and support. Today would be different. She was going to be in the thick of it. They drove to London. Mark knew that the synagogue had its own private car park where there would be space, and he would not have to feed a greedy meter somewhere.

Rabbi Hal came out to meet them as they parked, met Sue courteously, and led them into the main office building. They sat in Alec's room. Hal, pen in hand, heard the story from the beginning, Sue making timely contributions. At Mark's suggestion, they went downstairs into the basement to locate the records that would be important. He already knew where they were. This was his third visit to this private place and its layout was now very familiar. After an hour of delving, they brought three cardboard boxes up, taking them to Hal's car.

They separated then, to meet later. The gathering of the elders was a cheerful event. These people, all men, knew each other well. It was to be an occasion to consider a serious and worrying topic, but that did not prevent the emergence of lighthearted badinage here and there. Mark and Sue were warmly welcomed. If she, as the only lady present, was contravening some sort of traditional convention, then they did not show it, and she was made comfortable. Mark was invited to tell his story again, asked questions, and was included in their discussion about what measures should be taken. Inevitable conclusions emerged — we should see justice done and we are entitled to point the finger at Paul Jacobs. The synagogue did not otherwise have any share in the guilt, and we must be able to demonstrate that to the wider world.

At nine thirty the meeting broke up. Police involvement was seen as desirable, indeed inevitable, and they were to be informed, but Mark's cautions were understood, and nothing would happen without his agreement. Going to the law was not considered to be very urgent anyway. Over the next few days, Rabbi Hal and the group's lawyer would prepare a document, outlining the whole affair from the point of view of the synagogue. What might be done to correct the destiny of Kurt Feldman's estate would depend on what resulted from eventual police activity. It would rest there for the moment.

The documents had been examined by the meeting. It was agreed that the essential facts of the estate transactions, legal and improper, were now complete. However, there were minor omissions, two files on related matters that would clarify later explanations. Mark offered to go back into the basement now and recover them. Hal was to take him and Sue back to their car anyway. When they arrived in the yard again, Hal invited them to enter the office through the back of the temple where he and Mark had first chatted.

Sue was interested in Jewish ceremonial. This was her first venture into what were strange surroundings. They lingered in the office and the robing area while Hal explained something of the Jewish way of religious life, pointing out the Torah, and showing her the yarmulke, the skull cap on his head. Sue and Mark listened with fascinated respect. Despite the religious and cultural divide, they felt themselves becoming closer to this good man. It had been evident during the meeting that there was little to separate them from the elders of this community. At times, the differences evaporated in the exchange of friendly chatter — feelings were the same, the deity was the same, just an approach through different doors.

Mark excused himself, leaving Hal and Sue chatting, and said he would go to the basement and pick up the now easily located files. Hal nodded casually, knowing the Mark knew his way, and needed no guiding. He went through the temple door and began to make his way across to the access passage on the far side. Sufficient light was coming through the big windows from the street lamps outside to enable him to see. He smelled smoke — an acrid burning. He walked to the back of the hall, towards the large doors, supposing that the smell would be coming from the street. Then he saw flickering, high up, coming through the windows on the enclosed yard side.

He walked briskly to the passage archway. The door just beyond it was shut. He opened it. Now he could hear the sounds of a raging fire and the smell of burning intensified. There was thick smoke ahead of him looking down towards the reception. He ran on through. Darkness was no longer a problem. Two men were moving by the desk there, apparently rifling the drawers, pulling them out violently and letting them drop to the floor. In the noise and smoke Mark remained unnoticed almost until he reached them. The front door to the street was ajar. A third man was outside, peering in. A car stood on the double yellow lines, its doors open.

Mark knew what was happening. Flame was belching through the basement door area, and great gushes of thick smoke were pouring up the stair well. He grabbed a standard lamp from the desk as the man closest to him turned, warned by a shout from outside. Mark summoned up all his strength, swung the heavy brass lamp in a wide arc, and the base struck the man firmly on the side of the head. It crunched as it met the skull, and the man collapsed towards Mark, sliding off the edge of the desk to fall to the floor. The blood of a normally mild man was up now. It was hurt or be hurt. He suddenly felt confident. His caution of ten seconds ago had evaporated, to be replaced by fearless determination.

The other man was now advancing and he took hold of the lamp, wrenching it from Mark's grasp. Mark closed with him to limit his ability to raise it and strike. They grappled. The new opponent, cursing incoherently, pushing, trying to hook one of his legs round Mark's and overbalance him backwards. Mark instinctively allowed himself to retreat, grabbing one of the man's wrist in both his, ducking under and twisting to throw him off balance sideways. The man recovered from his crouch, coming at Mark again, reaching out to recover the only available weapon, the lamp. Mark kicked at him, aiming for his face, but finding his chest. This moved the man back. As he was losing his balance, Mark kicked again, catching him full in the face this time. Mark picked up the lamp, holding it at arms length behind him, ready to swing it again. The first man? Was he still a threat? No, he was motionless.

Mark turned now towards the street entrance. The door was wide open now. Someone shouted: "We have to go — come on!" Flame was leaping up the stair well, the heat becoming more intense, smoke thickening, the roar deafening in the confined space. Mark turned again towards his second target, now standing again, doubled up, one hand clutching at his face. A shout from the door again: "Come on! Come on!" The man looked at Mark cautiously, reassured to see that he was now moving back from the heat in the stair well, and was no longer a threat. He staggered to the door. In seconds the car revved loudly and was gone. Mark had now withdrawn to the passage, walking backwards, arms raised to fend off the heat, eyes half closed against the flaming brightness that the whole reception area had now become.

Hal was now in the passage way by the temple arch. He shouted: "Are you alright?"

Mark turned and put a hand to the Rabbi's shoulder. "Yes I think so — still standing anyway." They continued to retreat.

Hal shouted. "Sue is calling the fire brigade. There is nothing we can do there now. Come back across to the office and get away from it. You look rather tattered. There were men there?"

"Yes. Arsonists. No doubt about it. One of them is still there I think. I felled him, the bastard!"

They turned to look at the flames again. They had clearly taken firm hold in the first story of the old Victorian house now. Sue appeared, putting her arm through Mark's and looking at him with alarm.

"I'm okay. I'm okay" he shouted at her. They continued to move back and were now in the temple hall.

Sue said: "Help is on its way. I hope they are quick — that is really blazing now."

Hal said: "We can do nothing else for the moment. Let's go and move our cars away from the danger area if we can." His was closest to the burning building, and would be at risk. He was able to move it over into less danger. Mark's was already forty feet away. There was activity outside now. Sirens. The police were the first of the emergency services to arrive. They closed the connecting roads. There would be no moving in or out now. Hal went out to the road and identified himself to the nearest policeman, telling him where he could be found if needed. The flames raged. Crowds gathered. What could the three of them do? They watched, impotent, horrified.

Sue was the realist. She led Mark to the robing office. "Take your jacket off. It's a mess. There's blood on your hands, and on your cheek, and on your trousers." She looked closer. "Not yours apparently." She leant forward and kissed him. He was suddenly tired now, shivering with delayed reaction. Had he just killed a man? Obediently he raised his face. Sue, dampening tissues in the rest room hand basin, cleaned him up, checked him over, and looked at him carefully. He submitted to this meekly, and gratefully drank the glass of cold water that she handed him. She gave the same attention to Hal who was also paralyzed with shock. She said to him: "Is there anyone you would like to call? The phone still works."

He nodded, dropping his head, and moving to the desk. "My wife. She will be shocked. She will pass on the news to the people who matter." He was shivering now. Sue reached for his jacket, hanging over the back of his chair, and draped it over his shoulders. He raised his head briefly and nodded gratefully.

The fire brigade arrived noisily. One of the men appeared, asking where the electricity fuse box was. Hal showed him, and from then on they were in darkness. Within seconds, well-trained routines went into action. They fought the blaze from two directions, the street, and from the passage connecting the office to the temple, this hallowed area that was quickly to become a mess. Members of the Jewish community that lived locally began to arrive. Most were forbidden any access, but the determined were pointed in the direction of the temple office, using the back entrance, and were warned not to leave it. For two hours water was poured onto the conflagration. It was then apparent that the office building had burned out completely, and the house next door was badly damaged.

There was a sudden period of quiet, anti-climax, horror. People were standing round in the yard, motionless. What to do? Nothing could be done. Hal was fending off questions from anxious people arriving in a stream as the word had spread. He had no answers. It tested his patience. It showed.

Mark and Sue became by-standers. He had expected that there would be some sort of police or fire brigade enquiry under way now — were you here when it started? What did you see? Mark wondered whether he should have found someone in authority out there and told them that there had been a car, and at least four men. Well, so be it. It would all come out later. They wanted breathing space. Not until four thirty in the morning were they able to get consent to get their car out. They were going to leave chaos behind them.

Hal was a tattered and dejected man. Mark took him into the yard, now becoming quieter. "We are going now Hal. There is obviously nothing more that Sue and I can do to help for the moment."

"Well, for the record Mark, I think you were both magnificent. This will not be forgotten."

"And there is something else that should not be forgotten either, and that is why I wanted to have this last word with you. What we have just endured was arson. The fire was deliberately started. No doubt about it. And the instigators have now revealed themselves to us as our common enemy, the people at Celle. They are already aware of the danger that we represent to them. They have already identified me as a threat and warned me off as you know They had obviously decided that, apart from me and the information that came from Gunther Muller, the greatest risk to them lay in your archives, the estate transfer records that you were obliged by law to keep. They will now think that they have disposed of them. But what they will not be aware of, fortunately, is that we have already removed the important bits of it. We must not allow them to know that. Nothing must be said that suggests otherwise. If — for instance — you were to be asked by the press how extensive the loss was, tell them everything went. Nothing was saved. Then we get some breathing space."

Hal nodded. "Yes, I understand. You are going home?"

"It is just a shade past my bed time Hal. One more thing — we know that the police must remain involved soon, and last night's meeting accepted that. This fire may speed the process up. They will undoubtedly want to come and talk to you about a dead man in your reception, but we are not going to hang around awaiting the summons. When they want me, you can tell them where to find me. Okay?"

"Okay."

Mark and Sue headed north through suburban London, both exhausted by the night's events. The crossing of the motorway system put them close to a service area where they knew there would be a coffee and something to eat. They felt more relaxed now, secure and comfortable in each other's company. The passing of the night and the emergence of dawn as they drove on brought with it the usual renewal of energy. The pressure was off for the moment.

Sue's first routine on entering their house was to check for telephone messages. There were several of the social variety that could be deferred, but one demanded attention. She listened to it, and then clicked for a repeat, calling Mark to hear it. "Mr Woodford. This is Paul Jacobs, Alec's father. I am sorry not to have reached you, but I hope you will call me back as quickly as you can once you have heard this. I have come to London, and I am with my son. I need to talk to you urgently. Thank you." He gave a number that had a London code.

Mark sagged against the kitchen worktop, looking at Sue in disbelief. He checked the wall clock. Getting on for seven. Sunday morning! This was becoming a bit of a nightmare. He dialled the number. A hotel reception answered. Within seconds he was put through to Paul. Both his age and his anxiety were evident in his faltering voice. "Ah, Mr Woodford. Thank you for getting back to me. I do need to see you. It is most important. My son is here and we have a car. I do not want to bring you to London unnecessarily, but we could come out to you if convenient."

Mark was tempted to ask what it was all about, but knew that would be counter-productive. It was obviously going to have to be face to face. Ask them to come here? No. Not a safe thing to do now. He knew his mother would not mind if they met there. He gave Jacobs her address, telling him to be there at two in the afternoon, and giving him some helpful directions. It was time for rest and they went up and laid on their bed in companionable silence. So much had happened that sleep was elusive.

They lunched with Mark's mother. She told him that the television news had highlighted the synagogue fire, but there had been no mention of a body in the smouldering ruins, and no indication that arson was suspected. She was surprised to learn that they had both been there. Mark wondered whether they had somehow managed to extricate his victim, alive or dead. He thought dead, a chilling reality.

Paul and Alec Jacobs arrived promptly at two in the afternoon. Mark led them into his mother's library. This was very familiar, being the nook where he had poured over his books in his grammar school and undergraduate years. He and Sue made their guests welcome. They had made mother aware of the delicacy of this meeting and she happily made herself scarce. Paul was now a man in his seventies and looked it, spare and a little hunched, but bright eyed and articulate. Alec was just as Mark remembered him not many days ago, but whereas he had been confident the first time, he was now quiet and withdrawn, allowing his father to take the initiative.

Paul said: " Mr. Woodford. You are going to wonder why I have come to see you rather than say what I am about to say elsewhere. The reason is that you are clearly at the focal point of recent events that involve me and my son. It was apparent when you went to see him that you had discovered irregularities in the settling of the Feldman estate all those years ago. He passed onto me the details of you conversation, and I was, to some extent, responsible for the manner in which he dealt with you, including the letter he sent. We see you as a trustworthy and impartial person, involved in this for innocent reasons."

"The fact is that I have decided not to sustain any pretence that I had nothing to do with the problem. I have decided that I should admit to my part in the original wrongdoing. Several things are obvious now. You would agree with me and say that — yes — I have been found out. You would tell me that I would be hunted down, that not only would the police here and elsewhere have an interest in finding me, but that innocent people now known to you in Germany, the descendents of Kurt Feldman, would also like me to be brought to justice. I could, perhaps, have the option of hiding, trying to make myself invisible. However, I think that would be very difficult now."

He went on: "What is more important than that now is my conscience. At the time I worked with Heinrich Schwabl to gain all the wealth dishonestly, I had fallen into the trap of believing that I could turn my back on my religion, that the possession of wealth would be a substitute for the possession of faith, and that I could lead a happy life, and pass that happiness on to others. That has not proved to be the case Mr. Woodford. I can tell you that I have been unhappy during all these years. I was able to give my wife a settled existence, and she did not know the origins of my wealth, but now that she is dead I am not constrained by her presence."

"Apart from my own feelings, two things worry me now. I am an old man and I do not want to take guilt to my grave on two counts — one, the injustice done to good people in Germany who evidently still live, and have the legitimate right to Kurt Feldman's wealth — and the other, my son, who has been disadvantage by the limitations I have placed on his life. He has no guilt in this matter, and I now intend that he should become free to live as he wishes, whatever my fate may be now. It worried me greatly when I learned that he had tried to deceive you in order to keep you away from me. Enough is enough."

He bowed his head. Sue, surprised and impressed by his admissions, sensible of the delicacy of the moment, rose and walked over to the window.

Mark said to Paul: "Yes, we knew all about it. I do not fully understand why you have chosen to tell me this first, but I respect what you have said. I am supposing that you will be willing to talk to others in the same way. It will be as obvious to you as it is to me that the police are now going to involved inevitably, and they will want to talk to you. And the synagogue. They will be interested in your change of direction. But yours is a forgiving religion and I am sure they will want to welcome you back into their fold."

He went on: "Unfortunately, we have not had the same message of contrition from Germany. You will know that your original partner in this, Heinrich Schwabl, was already a prosperous hotelier when you first encountered him. His share of the estate went into his business which is now substantial. The problem for us is that, although he no longer lives, his son has turned out to be just as nasty. Did you know that the West London Synagogue was burned down last night?"

They were shocked. Paul said: "No. That is terrible news. A fire? You think Schwabl was involved?"

"Certainly. They wanted to permanently remove all the records from the basement there, believing that this act would reduce any possible threat to them."

Sue came to sit near Mark. She asked: "What do you want to do now, and how can we help?"

Alec said: "We wanted to tell someone that we felt we could trust to listen and understand. That is not always possible elsewhere. We did not know what was going on at the synagogue, what they would be thinking. We did not know to what extent the police had become involved. Father is rather infirm now, and I do not want him bundled into a cell somewhere. We thought that we should clear the matter with you, and then ask you kindly to let the essential people know how we think. One of the facts about the wealth is that, because of father's prudent management, It is still very substantial. We have no way of making reparation for the loss of the years, but we can give the money back."

The evident assumption of these two, father and son, that their principal fears should be of the attitudes of the police and the synagogue, worried Mark. He said to Paul:" What would Herr Schwabl think if he were here now, and had overheard our conversation?"

They were taken aback. Alec said: "How could he know that we were here?"

"I think you are missing the point. This man evidently arranged for the West London Synagogue to be raided last night, to remove a danger to him, records in the basement. It was a very deliberate and calculated act. He has demonstrated that he is prepared to be ruthless in eliminating sources of information pointing at him. You two are a source of information pointing at him. Simply by coming here and talking to us as you have, you have ratted on him. This man is bright, and the possibility of that will not have escaped him."

Mark leaned forward, emphasizing his words. "Do you really suppose that is had not crossed his mind that you are being pursued just as he is — that our discoveries spreading out from Gunther Muller incriminate you just as they do him, and that your capture and cross-examination by the police somewhere could lead to a confession that embraced his wrongdoings as well as your own? Come off it gentlemen. You are in potential danger."

They were silent. Thoughtful. "What should we do then?" asked Paul.

"Does anyone other than us know that you are in England, apparently in a London hotel?"

Paul shook his head. "No. We think not. We have had no contact other than you. Alec has his home here of course, in West London, but he has not been there for three days now."

"Then stay away from it. Leave us the hotel details, and go and mind your own business until you hear from me. Have no contact with anyone. No reunions with friends, no sightseeing, just stay put. I will be in touch, or, if I think appropriate, some one else will be. It may be several days."

That was that. Mother appeared gracefully with the formula tray of English afternoon tea, cucumber sandwiches, and chocolate cake. A little later the Jacobs left to go back to London.

They migrated to the kitchen. Muffin was everywhere. Mother had been in her lounge and had caught the up-to-the-minute television news. They had found a body at the synagogue, death by asphyxiation. She knew Mark and Sue had been there, but was unaware of the crisis that was growing as a result. They did not enlighten her for the moment.

Mark was relieved that he was not being connected with the death, but he was beginning to feel less sensitive about it all anyway. Last night he had experienced the natural horror of a law-abiding man suddenly finding himself the cause of someone else's demise. Now he was becoming inured. He wondered how Hal was faring and what was happening there.

What to do now? The police would be hoping to talk to him?. Their first concern would be the fire, but what about the wider affair? He envisioned long consultations, statements, a slow gathering of information. The British police could not act in Celle. They would have to consult with their opposite numbers. More talk.

Had Hal mentioned him yet? Where would the next hammer blow from Celle fall? He and Sue discussed it fully. They were in danger of course. How could they not be. They would be traceable. Were the sisters and Helmut safe in Halle? Probably not now. It was reasonable to suppose that the Schiller organization would go to any lengths to preserve its business from scandal, including some homicide on the way if it suited them.

They had to make decisions. They had to take the initiative. They made several 'phone calls from mother's kitchen. The first was to Sue's surgery. She had a straightforward chat to her boss, revealing her involvement in matters relating to the London synagogue fire now in the news, and told him briefly about the Gunther Muller discovery and the problems it had unleashed. She asked for their tolerance in allowing her to be off work for a few days while she helped Mark to deal with the police, and to straighten things out elsewhere. They agreed unreservedly.

Helmut was at work when Mark called Halle. He was able to ask Lise if she was well. Had anyone been in touch with them in a way that worried them? No. All was quiet.

Mark had hoped to be able to have a short chat with Hal, to find out what was happening there, but he could get no answer from the synagogue now. Perhaps this good man was at home having a well-deserved rest, something that Mark and Sue believed was overdue for them now also. With mother, they walked Muffin along the ridge for some precious fresh air, and were her guests for the night. Everything would have to wait until they had replenished their energies.

13

Back home the next morning, Mark had expected some sort of overture from the police, telephone call, message, please call us? He heard nothing. He wondered why, but not for long. Ha called Hal, now back picking up the pieces at the synagogue and had an explanation.

"It has all been rather surprising Mark," said Hal. "There was an inspector here for about an hour this afternoon. We had a chat in the temple office first, and then a wander through the passage. We could not go into what remains of the main building because there is still danger there, and they have put up those yellow plastic ropes as barriers. I told him about our suspicions that it may have been started deliberately, mentioning the Feldman affair."

"He was not interested?"

"No, quite simply. Out of consideration for you I did not mention Gunther Muller. I did not think there was any need. After all, from our point of view, although we knew about the Schwabl Jacobs fraud from our connection with you, we have been able to discover from our own researches that you were right. How you learned about it should be your business, not ours. Anyway, this man heard me out about the estate and the 1955 advertisement, and then stopped me from going further. He asked me if we had suffered any loss as a result. When I told him no, he said that in that case he doubted whether they would be looking into it. It was all too long ago."

"Good heavens Hal, that's incredible. And I have been waiting for them to knock on the door at any moment with a handful of penetrating questions. Did he not mention the man lying in the reception?"

"Yes. But that is not going to involve you either. He was dead of course, but they had another explanation for his demise — accidental. They had discovered that there had been some interference with the main electrical switchboard in the basement. Some of the fuses had been taken out, intended to take power away from any intruder alarm systems they think, and there was evidence that this led to the fire. Their theory, and they are sticking to it, is that this man broke in as a common burglar, opening one of the basement windows, and then opening the main door to an accomplice outside. They had no particular interest in the basement, but rifled all the drawers and cupboards elsewhere, including in the office upstairs. Apparently, they say, there is evidence of them having done that despite the fire damage. They think that when the fire took hold, and the heat in the stair wells was intensifying, your man was trapped upstairs. He somehow managed to fall from the landing on the first floor. He hit the desk in the reception below, cracking his head."

Hal, forty miles away, could not see Mark shaking his head in wonderment, but he was doing so. "This is astonishing Hal. You and I are privy to what must be the biggest financial crime of the century, and they are turning a blind eye."

"Well, I cannot say that I am affronted by it. It would have been nice to see a just end to the Feldman business, but my first concerns are here. We have a hell of a mess as you know. At least we are fully insured, and I am not short of help this morning. How are you Mark, and Sue? Have you recovered from all the excitement?"

"We're okay Hal, thanks. We did have a surprise call that you should know about though, and I think this is a good time to tell you. We had a message when we got home yesterday from Paul Jacobs."

There was silence for a moment, puzzlement. "He called you? That was the last thing we may have expected. What did he want?"

"What he wants is to be able to repair the damage he caused. He has had a change of heart. Honestly repentant. He is in London at the moment, with Alec, and on my advice they are keeping themselves out of the way. They came up here yesterday afternoon and we met at my mother's place. He has had enough. He wants to give the money back. He says that these years since he did the deed have not been happy, and, anyway, he knows that there would be a search for him. He says that he now regrets having turned his back on his religion, and all your traditions, and just wants to get back close to your community and restore what he can of the wealth back to the people in Germany."

"Well. Good. I am surprised, but delighted, of course. And here we have been imagining that he would be hard to find. We have been uncertain about his whereabouts. Alec always said that his father had settled in Israel, but we never knew where, and, according to him, neither did he. Still, it is good news for the sisters in Germany if he is going to repay it all, and at least we are not going to have to suffer some bad publicity. We have had a great fear, since our meeting the other night, that if the newspapers got hold of the scandal, we would have a difficult problem."

He went on: "What about the value of Paul's part of the estate now? Presumably it is much reduced. He must have spent a lot of it."

"Not so apparently. He is a financially aware person and has been prudent with it all. The amount that is now available to pass on to the sisters is about the same as they would have expected it to be if they had inherited it in the usual way."

"Good. And what does Alec think about it all?"

"He goes along with it. He was not in on the original sin as it were, and, although he did become involved in the deceits a bit by trying to divert me when we met the first time, he agrees with his father's intentions."

"We must talk to them."

"That is the proper thing to happen Hal. I will get Paul to give you a ring."

"You will pass on the news to the sisters in Germany?"

"Probably. There would be sense in them meeting with Paul and Alec. It would be a simple transfer between him and them, and they could decide between them how it should be done. It will only be half of what they are due, but it is obviously going to be a fortune anyway, and it is going to change their lives, and their children's. They will be pleased. Who knows, they may have a lenient attitude and let Paul off lightly in view of his change of heart, leaving him with somewhere to live perhaps, and it reverts to them after he is gone."

Hal changed the subject: "Mark. I think you should know that we had some press here yesterday, and more today. This has been just about the fire, and nothing to do with Feldman. I have been telling them about the police conclusions, and not mentioning any doubts I may have about their validity. I just wanted to tell you that I have born your advice in mind. I have been telling them that everything was lost, and that is how it will appear in the papers I hope and expect. Do you think that we are still threatened?"

"One thing is certain. They are going to be very much on their guard in Celle. They will be aware of what appears in the London papers, and they will be encouraged by reports confirming that all was lost in the fire. That was their objective. But they will not consider that they are completely in the clear yet, not by a long way. We have been thinking that we are one step ahead of them in this game of wits, but we may not be. They are a canny bunch, and our worry must focus less on the predictable, and more on the unexpected. My mind is in a continuous process of evaluation and prediction, but I am not encouraged by the results. With a little more insight I may have seen fit to warn you that a raid on your records was likely, but I missed out on it."

"Worrying. And Paul is obviously vulnerable. From what you say, he is changing sides — telling all. If they knew that they would be after him. Is he in danger?"

"Who can say. I imagine that they think him safe. Paul's repentance is surprising us, and it would surprise them. I doubt if he has become a target yet."

They ended their conversation with affection and mutual respect that, if had been universal, would have put the whole world at peace.

Mark told an expectant Sue about this conversation. She had heard half of it anyway, sipping coffee at their kitchen table. She was pleased that Hal was happy to talk to Paul and Alec.

Mark rang Helmut in Halle. This was Monday and they knew it was his regular day off. "Hi Helmut. How are you, and the ladies?"

"We are well Mark. But we have been worrying about you and what you may be doing."

"We are okay. Helmut, I have some news for you, and also some more warnings."

"Go on."

"You are well aware that Schwabl and his hoodlums at Celle know of Lise and Helga, and of your permanent connection to these two possible risks to the secrecy of their Feldman fraud."

"Yes, of course."

"Helmut, we have been perhaps a little too casual about the risks to you. I can tell you it is likely that you are safe for the moment, because Celle has been taking some deliberate action to safeguard themselves, and they are going to believe that they are succeeding. However, if anything happens that indicates to them that they are vulnerable in other areas, then they may take very deliberate action to remove the threat."

Mark paused. Helmut was listening intently. "Let me give you give you the news first. the great grandfather's estate was divided into two. The elder Schwabl had half, and the other half went to the administrator at the West London Synagogue. This man, Jacobs, in a moment of sinful diversion, saw through the attempt by Schwabl to claim the money, and demanded that he get half. So it was. Well, Jacobs, still alive and living in America, has discovered that we are on his tail as well as on Schwabl's. But instead of heading for cover, he has decided to come out into the open and return the money, and it will shortly be available for the sisters."

"Oh — my goodness. That is wonderful. Wait a moment while I tell Lise..."

Mark yelled down the 'phone: "No. Not yet Helmut — hear me out."

"Okay. Sorry."

"You must understand that there would be great danger for you all if you were suddenly to display signs of wealth. You are known to Schwabl. He thinks of you as a head waiter, doing a dependable job for him locally, and loyal to his cause. They must be watching you quietly. It is extremely important that you do not change your lifestyle there one bit. You are going to have funds before long that will change your lives completely. You will be able to go and buy a nice country house somewhere, do some traveling, go into a comfortable retirement. And all your extended family are going to be able to improve the comfort of their lives. But it must not happen yet, and you are going to be just as positive with Lise and Helga about this as I am being with you. Do you understand?"

"Yes. Yes, of course."

"You may be wondering why I am giving you this news now. You may think I could just have sat on it for the time being. Well, there is a reason to involve you. This man Jacobs is in London now. I do not need to tell you that his presence here is dangerous, particularly as he has changed sides. I am anxious to get him together with you and the sisters a soon as possible so that some arrangements can be made to transfer the wealth to you. If Schwabl were to find out that he is here, and is allying himself to the enemy, then he could be dealt with in a very final way. If that were to happen before he has signed some checks and set up the transfers, then you may never get your hands on it."

"I understand."

"Now. You and Lise are local there in Halle, but Helga will not be watched so closely, if at all. I want you to send her here to London, on her own. She will need to bring banking details, and you will trust her to act on behalf of you all. She will act as the go-between, and well as one of the beneficiaries. We will get her together with the Jacobs. I will vouch for her as your representative. She will only need to be here for one night and will stay with us. When she goes back she will be in full possession of all that you need to know about accessing half the estate. The whole amount will not arrive immediately. It may take a number of months, and involve both you and the Jacobs with lawyers, but that will not matter very much."

"Okay. I will organize that. She will come. When Mark?"

"Best if you talk to her, and then ring me back. My German is not up to a complex conversation yet. Find out when she could come, and then I will check out the arrangements at this end. But not a word to anyone outside the family Helmut. And warn all your children — total secrecy."

14

Hal rang at ten the following morning. "Sorry to keep bothering you Mark. Just to tell you that we think we had a couple of snoopers around last night. One of my assistants saw what he thought was torchlight coming from the ruined building when he drove passed at about ten thirty. We do not need to be alarmed do we?"

Mark thought. "Well. Who knows? Perhaps the enemy are surveying their success. It would not surprise me now."

"Okay. Well, that was all."

"Actually Hal. I am glad you called, because I was going to give you a ring sometime this morning. I want to ask you to cooperate in a diversion that I have in mind. One of our joint worries is our ignorance of what is going through the minds of the people in Celle. They have made their raid, and they are assuming for the moment that it was successful. And they have left me alone, which has surprised me rather. So it is not unreasonable for us to assume that we are ahead of the game."

He went on: "However, that is a dangerous assumption. Schwabl, owning several hotels in England, and two in London, obviously has local people here he can call on to act as fire-raisers, thugs, spies and infiltrators, and the villains the other night were shouting to each other in English, not German. So we cannot think of them as a distant enemy — they are very local. And the presence of Paul Jacobs is worrying me."

"I have in mind a way of softening the atmosphere a bit. I believe that, at this point, I am trusted. What I want to do is to call Celle and speak to my contact man there, and give him information that will suggest to him that I am on their side. If I can then back up that information cleverly, then not only will their trust in me will be reinforced, but they will be reassured about other things that may be bothering them."

"So, Mark, what are you proposing to do, and how can we help?"

"Celle think that their fire demolished all the records. They would be impressed if I were to tell them that I have found out otherwise — that you had been through the basement before the fire and located all the damaging documents. I could tell them that I know where they are now being kept, and how to get at them. This would impress them. There would be no risk to you, but their confidence in me would be increased, and that would reduce, or at least delay, the inevitable eventual realization that the army facing them is led by General Mark Woodford. It would give us time to deal with the Jacobs and get him out of the way. I have asked the Bormanns to send one of the sisters over as soon as possible, so that the transfer of half the estate can be set up face to face with Jacobs, as it needs to be. I am waiting to hear. It will be Helga."

"You know, of course," said Hal, "that this change in policy would be in denial of our public declarations that everything was lost."

"That should not worry us. Celle would not have expected you to openly declare that their documents had been put safely to one side. They must be supposing that the West London Synagogue now has knowledge of the fraud. What I am suggesting takes the pressure off of you as well as me."

"How do we do it?"

"Copy all the documents as soon as possible, and put the copies somewhere safe. Then put the originals in three cardboard boxes and put them in the passage leading from the ruins of the office to the temple. Put some other stuff in there, janitorial things, a couple of bicycles, move a filing cabinet out there with innocent papers in it."

"Are we not parting with precious and essential evidence if we allow them to get the papers?"

"No. I don't think that they matter too much any more. Paul Jacobs knows it all and he will tell it all. So long as you have copies we are going to be able to clear this matter up. Our strength now is that we know Jacobs is coming clean, but Celle does not. I need to contrive to retain their confidence in me and my conformity to their wishes. I have to get the pressure off."

"You say that Paul Jacobs will tell it all. I am sure he will, but what do we do with the information? You have, I know, had reservations about making total disclosures to the police. Breaking into that hotel in Munich for one thing, accepting that bribe — temporary or not — killing a man not fifteen yards from where I am sitting. Not only that, but if the Bormanns are forgiving to Jacobs, which I am sure they will be if they are to get their money in full, then we would not want this repentant man to spend his declining years in prison. My impression of your approach to this whole problem has been that we will see justice done without depending on the law to achieve it."

"That remains true. What I hope for is a detailed account from Paul Jacobs, outlining in full how the fraud was committed and who was involved. We would want that notarized legally. Then, after we have removed him to somewhere safe, we would make that information available to the Bormanns, and suggest that they find a good lawyer in Germany who can sue Schwabl in the normal civil way. If this man were to find a lawyer on his doorstep, acting within the proper parameters, representing a large and well-known company, then he would have to fall into line. There would be no question of him burning down a few more offices. The finger of suspicion would point straight at him if there was to be any stepping out of line in a violent or criminal way."

"Okay Mark. I will go along with that. So we are to be raided again?"

"Yes, probably. I will tell Celle that your complex there will be unoccupied between the hours of ten in the evening, and eight in the morning."

"Right. Give me until tomorrow night and I will have it all done and in place."

"Thanks Hal. Do you and your wife take a drink?"

"We have been known to thicken our heads with a glass of good wine when the occasion has justified it."

"Good. Then we are going to crack a good bottle when this is all over."

"Why not. The occasion will certainly justify it."

Mark sat and thought for a while. Sue was at work which he regretted. She was always a valuable bouncing target for ideas. Still, there was another 'phone call to make now. He dialed the Schiller Group in Celle, and had himself put through to Gustav.

"Herr Richter. Good morning."

"Ah. Mr. Woodford. How are things with you?"

"Just a little confused I am afraid. I thought I should ring you with an update of what is happening here, some of it a little disturbing."

"Please go on."

Well. I have been in close touch with the synagogue in the last couple of days. They regard me as a friend, and they talk to me if anything crops us concerning the Feldman affair. The good news for the moment in that they seem not to be worrying about pursuing it in your direction. I think you may know that they had a very serious fire a couple of nights ago that demolished their office building, and just about everything in it. I think that was certainly your work was it not?"

"Does it matter whose work it was then Mr. Woodford?"

'Not to me, but I have thought that you would have good reason to want to dispose of any files that were in their storage. If it was you who organized it then you will now be thinking that you succeeded."

"Are you telling me that it was not successful?"

"It was not entirely successful. I have found out that on the afternoon preceding the fire, certain records relating to the Feldman estate and the setting up of the trust, were removed from the basement. There was going to be a meeting of the elders next day, and they were to have a look at them."

"And they did so?"

"No. The fire happened that night and they have all been involved in the result of that. There is a terrible mess there and it is going to take them many days to clear it up. They were telling me earlier that they are unlikely to get around to any normal administration tasks for at least another week."

"Even so. The fire did not help us much did it?"

"It may not have done you much harm Herr Richter, because my main reason for calling you is to tell you that I know where the three boxes of documents are being stored for the time being, and it would be easy for you to take them if you wished."

"Could you get these boxes for us Mr. Woodford?"

"That would be a very dangerous thing for me to try. I am known there to start with, and I am not an expert at this sort of activity. And I have my work to think of. If I was caught out in some sort of illegal act, it would be hard for me to explain to my employers. I have hoped that you would have some way of organizing it without my active help."

"I understand. Perhaps we can deal with it. Where are the boxes?"

"There is a passageway leading from the temple to the reception on the ground floor of the office building. The old building is now severely damaged of course, but the passage is still there and undamaged at the temple end. Because they have a serious storage problem now, they are using the passage to keep things in. The three boxes are there, amongst a lot of other stuff, but easy to identify. Whoever went in to get them would have to duck under some safety barriers that have been put round the front of the building, but there are no locks, just a need to step through fallen masonry."

"And when would be the best time to go for them?"

"At any time between ten in the evening and eight in the morning. There is no one there at between those times."

"Well. Thank you for telling me."

"One more thing Herr Richter. You have not admitted to me that you did arrange for the office building to be burned, and it is none of my business anyway, but I should tell you that the police here have no interest in the fire. They think it was caused by an electrical fault during a burglary. A body was found in the reception area after the fire had been put out, and they believe that this man fell from the first floor landing when it became impossible to use the stairs. They think that he was an intruder looking for anything he could find to spend on drugs or whatever. And the synagogue has no reason to dispute that conclusion."

"So, Mr. Woodford. If no one else suspects us as the cause of the fire, why do you?"

"Only because it fits in so well with what I know about your concerns. I am pleased that it happened of course, because of my commitment to you, having accepted your payment. If those records threaten you then they threaten me indirectly. I gave you an assurance that I would make things safe for you over here, and removing them would help."

"Thank you. Tell me, did the police identify the man who died in there?"

"Yes. I understand he was a London man. He was carrying some identification, but I do not know his name or anything about him."

They brought their conversation to an end amicably. Mark felt odd about it all, consorting with the enemy. Taking the money in Celle had worried him, but there was no alternative. At least he had been able to act as if he was committed to them. He regretted somewhat that they should think it possible of him. Well. All in a good cause.

More telephoning had to be done. His ears were burning. Helmut rang to say that Helga could come over tomorrow if that could be fitted in. Mark rang Paul's hotel and found him in, cautious and hesitant. Yes, he would make himself available, with Alec, for a meeting at two in the afternoon.

Mark went through to their computer and put it on line. The search engine offered him a list of German law firms that had London offices. He picked one at random, a large company that had numerous offices in Germany, and branches elsewhere across Europe. He rang them, and was put through to a man who was obviously English. "I need a lawyer to attend a meeting in West London tomorrow afternoon.

This meeting is between an American who has considerable wealth, and wishes to transfer a large proportion of it to a German family, settlement of an old debt. A lady member of the family will be here to deal with the matter of their behalf. Our requirement is to ensure that the set up of transfer procedures is done in a legal contractual way, so that both sides understand how they are to proceed. This is very short notice, but if you can do this for me, your man should have fluent German. I will be responsible for the cost."

"No problem. We can do that." Mark offered personal information, and it was arranged.

Mark had another question. "This matter does not involve any dispute, but there is an element of confidentiality. I must ask you if you are, or have been, retained as lawyers for any German hotel groups?"

"Do you have one in particular in mind?"

"Yes. Let's look at it another way. Can you tell me who you act for?"

"No reason why not. Hang on a moment." He was obviously going into his own computer, and came back a few seconds later. "We are not currently retained by any hotel groups in Germany as such, nor do we appear to have been in the recent past, at least fifteen years. There have been a number of one-off assignments, usually property transfers, but these have only involved smallish companies, not a large groups. The fact is, of course, that large companies usually have, and need, legal departments of their own. Our business tends to provide a service for smaller organizations and individuals." Good, thought Mark. So long as you are not a part of the Schiller team, then we are safe. They left it at that.

Back to Helmut again. Mark would meet Helga at London Airport, go with her to the Kensington hotel, stay for the meeting, and then bring her to their home. All was arranged. Mark did not mention the lawyer. The importance of his presence would not be so obvious to him. Meeting the cost? Mark had their money in his bank, and would explain it all later.

Helmut had more to say. "I have a surprise. I do not know how important it might be. I have been reading the diaries of Kurt Feldman quietly in the mornings before I go to work. Lise does not bother very much, and I just pass on to her things that are interesting. You can imagine that most of it, the day-to-day accounts of his business life, is rather repetitive, historic or not. But it is interesting. He had an extraordinary life, this man, and, apart from anything else, I am sure that there could be a very good book based on his life story. There are some things that have turned out to be surprising, and also shocking. And I should tell you about one of those things."

"Back at the turn of the century, when Kurt Feldman's father was still alive, their main business was butchery. One of the tasks that the father gave Kurt was to go and look for good farms that they could buy, places that would be right for cattle and sheep rearing. Apparently, being Jewish, they had less interest in pigs of course, and the diary makes that clear. So Kurt traveled, and one of his wandering journeys was to the region where Celle is. They already intended to open some retail shops there. At this time Kurt had not met or married his wife, who was to become the mother of Johann."

"So, as Kurt describes, he arrived in Celle, and there was already a butchers shop in the town. So he had to decide whether they would open another one and compete, or whether they would make an offer for the existing shop and take it over. Well, he talked to them, and their name was Schwabl he says. It was a couple in their early fifties. He stayed in the area for a while, going to other towns nearby as part of the same search. We know he was there for several weeks anyway, because you can follow the dates of the diary entries."

Mark was listening carefully. Helmut's English was very good, interspersed with Americanisms because of his service with them at *Friesinger*, but one did have to pay close attention.

Helmut went on: "Anyway, the Schwabls had a daughter, and she and Kurt became close. However, the family knew that he was Jewish and they would not permit any sort of relationship to develop. So, Kurt and the girl used to get together secretly, and he must have been a determined young man because she became pregnant. Kurt had to go back to Hamburg of course, to report to his father, and they did open another butcher's shop in Celle. Kurt makes it clear that his father did not like the idea of a gentile daughter-in-law, so there was not much help from him, even though he must have thought differently when another young gentile lady appeared in Kurt's life as we know."

"Things did not change very much it seems when it became known that the girl was pregnant. She just went on and had the baby. But Kurt did want to take some responsibility for it. They were prosperous anyway, and the father agreed that she could have some financial support, including buying her a small house in Celle. So it was. Well, the baby was Heinrich Schwabl, and we have to accept the evident truth, that the Schwabl we now see as the evil man in Celle, was son of the half brother of Johann."

Mark was astonished. "This is just incredible. Incredible! What a tangle we are in. What else can possibly emerge to surprise us? Does our living Schwabl know of this connection Helmut? Does the diary give a clue to that?"

"It is not specific. The Schwabl family apparently just allowed the girl to rear the lad as if he was legitimate. That must have been difficult for them in those puritanical times. They did not want to acknowledge the Jewish connection. However, Kurt remained supportive for a number of years. Eventually he took over his father's business when he died, expanding into shipbuilding and the rest as we know. He eventually bought the *Uhland* estate at Celle. Meanwhile, without anyone except the butcher's daughter knowing, he paid for the boy to be educated, and then, in indirect and secret ways, helped him to go into a partnership to start a land agents business in Celle. He then used him as the agent to run his estate. It appears that he was often absent from it of course, so he needed someone. And it is clear from the diary that he never revealed to the young man that he was his father. We suppose that the young mother forbade that. She was to die in the early thirties, but it is evident that Kurt kept the secret after she had gone. Perhaps by then, with a happy marriage, and a son of his own becoming successful in the hotel business in Munich, he did not want to complicate his life."

Mark said: "This is astonishing Helmut. And it is surprising in another way. We have supposed from the start of all this, that the elder Schwabl, your little boy, had access to the papers at the *Uhland* estate because he had the trust of Feldman, and was able thereby to get such a wealth of information about Kurt and his business, that he took over *Friesinger* without any resistance when he went down there. We know that *Uhland* was bought in Johann's name, that Feldman told him to take it over in 1938, and that he was worried about the Jewish connection and stayed away. This absence gave Schwabl the opportunity to submerge himself in the estate, effectively adopting it in his own right. How could it be then that he missed out on the diaries? They were there. If he had read them, he would know that he was the illegitimate son of Kurt."

Helmut said slowly: "Perhaps he did know. Perhaps his determination to take over *Friesinger* resulted form his knowledge that he was Kurt's son. Perhaps he resented the legitimate line of descent and decided to do away with them. It would explain the violent way in which he did it. He would have known that there was immense wealth in the Feldman family. He may have disapproved of his mother's and his grandparent's resistance to a marriage. Perhaps he lived in a state of perpetual hate."

Mark thought that was likely. "And he would not have hesitated to go for the 1955 chance to grab the wealth, would he?"

Sue came in, and Mark ended his conversation with Helmut. Their business had been done for the moment. He brought her up-to-date, finishing with the diary disclosures. She said: 'They must wonder in Celle where those diaries are now. We know from the letter found on Gunther that the father had sent someone up to *Uhland* to get them, along with all the other stuff, and they ended up in the nook in *Friesinger*. That nook was unknown to father Schwabl, otherwise he would have cleared it, and therefore it was unknown to his son."

Mark said: "Does this alter our attitude to Schwabl in any way?"

"I don't see how. What the father did was thoroughly evil, the son knows it, is benefiting from it, and has shown no sign of wanting to make the same sort of restoration as the Jacobs are doing. If Max

Schwabl knows that there were diaries once, and has, presumably, wondered where they ended up, do we gain another weapon? If you were to give them a clue that diaries had been found, would that be an additional inducement to Schwabl to come to London and recover them? Is there an element of shame in his thinking, disgrace? Resent that his father should have conceived wantonly? We know that they fear publicity as well as police interest. Does Schwabl have the sort of pride that would be severely dented by a disclosure in his own social circles that his origins were less than respectable?"

Mark said: "Well, what we have learned from Helmut has explained much, but I think it helps us little. Schwabl is an evil man, and we do not have to speculate about the reasons. Just put a stop to him."

Helga arrived as arranged the next afternoon. Mark had suffered the difficulties of the Heathrow Airport complex to meet her — congestion, noise, and impatience. They made their way to the hotel for the meeting, chatting in a hesitant way. Helga told him that she would be going back to Munich that night, assuming that an overnight stay would not be necessary. Mark understood. This German lady was on her own, felt vulnerable and alone probably, and would be happier returning to her own familiar environment.

The meeting went as hoped and predicted. Paul looked worn and anxious, and these symptoms of fear were evident in Alec also. However, they were cooperative, and Paul was able to explain his affairs in an orderly way. The lawyer took notes, and it was clear that there would have to be further contact between his company and the Bormanns. This would happen in Halle. A substantial amount of cash was paid on the spot in the form of a cheque. There was a considerable amount of property and investments to deal with.

How would Paul survive? They came to a compromise. He knew exactly how much he had gained from the original share-out with Schwabl senior. He had been very prudent in the management of the assets down the years, and the current equivalent value, worked out to a formula accepted by all present as valid, amounted to somewhat more than that due to the Bormanns. A residual amount was calculated, and he would keep that. It was not insubstantial.

Under the lawyer's direction, Paul conferred administration rights to Alec, so that he would have the authority to make the transfers at intervals locally from London. So it ended, and Mark took Helga back to Heathrow Airport.

He headed north. His mobile buzzed on the seat beside him. It was Sue. Gustave Richter had rung him at home, and said it was urgent that they talk. Sue was fearful and it showed in her voice. Mark thought that this was the dreaded end. What had he done that was causing alarm over there? They had been so careful to disguise those of their actions that diverted from Celle's known hopes.

Wait until he got home? No, deal with it now. He looked at his watch. Mid evening, so it could not be office hours at *Uhland*, but, he had said it was urgent. Give it a try. He pulled off the motorway into a service area and called. It was Gustav himself who answered.

"Mr. Woodford. I am glad that you have called me back so promptly. Your wife said you were off at your college getting ready for the new session. I need to talk to you urgently."

"Carry on Gustav. I am in no particular rush."

"Not on the telephone. In person. There are things I need to discuss with you, and there is a need for absolute confidentiality."

"Have I stepped out of line somehow Herr Richter? In which case..."

"No. Not at all as far as I know. In fact I can tell you that Herr Schwabl was very pleased to hear of your information regarding the location of the boxes at the synagogue. However, the need to talk to you face-to-face remains. Can you come over here? How committed are you for the next twenty-four hours?"

Mark was out of the car, stretching his legs. The come and go of the service area was busy about him, engine sounds, bright light, chat, movement. And here he was contemplating disaster, with an anguished wife, and what he was now interpreting as a veiled threat from the most dangerous source in his life. It was becoming too much, but there could be no escape.

"Okay. If it is that urgent. Do you want me to come to Celle? I will need to book myself onto a flight."

"No need Mr. Woodford. There is a flight out of Heathrow to Hamburg tomorrow morning at eleven-fifty, and I have a reserve on a seat for you. I can confirm that locally here immediately. Would that work for you?"

"Yes."

"I shall not be there to meet you personally, but I will have a car and driver there. Because you will not know each other, I will have the driver ask for a public address call for you, and that will tell you where to find him."

"If you are arranging for the flight, how do I get the ticket?"

"Just go to the enquiry desk of Deutscher Airlines at Heathrow an hour before the flight. They will be expecting you."

There could be no speculating for the sudden reason for this summons. Mark and Sue thought through all the recent past and its complications. Yes, there were many possibilities of dangerous revelation to Celle. And yes — Mark had stepped out of line very deliberately. They had a restless night.

Mark arrived in Hamburg as planned, and made contact with the driver, who was courteous and affable. They drove for an hour, passing through the town of Celle, almost within sight of the *Uhland* Mansion, and then into the quieter country beyond. The driver turned into a driveway and they pulled up at the front door of an attractive house, set in an isolated spot, and surrounded by fir trees. Gustav Richter was immediately on his doorstep, beckoning Mark to enter. The car departed.

He led the way through into a lounge. A lady was there whom he introduced as his wife Olga. She smiled agreeably, welcomed him in good English, enquiring about his journey. Had he eaten today? She hoped he would take some lunch with them a little later, but meanwhile a coffee would be welcome? Would he like an opportunity to wash his hands after his journey?

Mark was surprised. This was not the hard face of the Schiller Organization. It was almost as if they were old friends. Gustav waved him to a comfortable armchair, and took one himself. "It is Mark is it not? Let us have a little less formality." He folded his hands in front of him, almost as if he was in prayer, lowered his head in thought for a moment, and then looked at Mark eye to eye.

"The first thing I must tell you is that Max Schwabl is now in London. He was in the air going one way as you were coming the other. The second thing I must tell you is that this conversation between us is, and will remain, unknown to him, and that is why I asked you to come across to see me here. There was no way I could come to see you in England, because my continuous presence is a feature of my position with Schiller, and, if I were to be absent without a valid explanation, then I would focus some suspicion on myself."

Olga came in with coffee and served it delicately. Gustav waited while she did so, and then waved her to another chair to join them. Clearly, she had been briefed that this would happen, and sat attentively.

Gustav continued: "We have one difficulty between us Mark, and that is establishing trust. The reason I have asked my wife to join us is so that you will recognize our honesty. If I were talking to you in a bar somewhere, then we are both on our guard, but here, in our home, with a companion who is obviously not an assassin, I am hopeful that you will see valid and good honest reasons for what I am about to tell you, and will have no personal inhibitions." He glanced at this wife. "Olga and I have been happily married for more than twenty-five years, and we are now grandparents. She is partly responsible for you being here. She shares my distaste for the bad things at Schiller, and that has led to inviting you here."

"The fact is that, in the matter of the Feldman estate, I have sympathies that parallel yours. I can reveal to you that, although I have been with the Schiller group for nearly thirty years, I have not been able to live with the knowledge of that distant crime comfortably. But most of the time is has not mattered. For most of the time we have simply operated as a hotel group, a growing company driven along by professional management, just the normal day-to-day routines of any commercial organization."

"However, from time to time, that blot in our history has reared its head. Let me tell you how I first knew of it. I joined Schiller as an accountant, and, going back then, it was necessary to indulge in some deceits about the group finances when we were dealing with the tax authorities. Heinrich was about in person then at the top of the company, and he had no option but to put me in the know about the Feldman connection, and the London fraud. He was able to soften it rather, to making it seem less criminal, but we knew it was illegal to say the least. Thus I became part of the inner circle that was in the know."

"I must admit now that I have always shrugged my shoulders a little. I was trusted always, then as now. They have always looked after me well and I have demonstrated my loyalty often. So, I have just gone along with it."

Mark turned to Olga. "Did you know about it too?"

She nodded. "Yes. I knew as soon as Gustav did I think, and it has been a handicap for both of us."

"Anyway," continued Gustav, "I am now having to come to terms with what is happening. It embarrassed me greatly to have to meet you and bribe you. And it is no less of an embarrassment to have to talk to Max as regularly as I do, and act out the part of an accomplice. I am getting deeper into it, and I have decided that I must do something to get out of it."

For Mark, this encounter was becoming comforting. He could not see any possible way in which this meeting could turn out to be a planned strategy to advantage Max Schwabl's position. He listened carefully.

"Your case is a strong one Mark. I do not see how we can wriggle out from under it in anything approaching a legal way. Max is, on the one hand, a clever man and a bright businessman, but on the other he has inherited his father's ruthlessness. I can tell you for certain that if he cannot deal with this Feldman thing in clever and deceitful ways, then he will resort to violent ones. He has done it before."

"He has done it before?"

"Yes. Seven years ago he murdered two people in Saxony. The

man was an elderly widower, and we had a half share in his hotel at that time. It was only a small place, but there was a lot of land involved, and room for expansion. We now own it. Well, Max had a meeting with him to try and get agreement to a complete buy out. This man was reluctant to go ahead with it at the offered price. So Max made a different approach, the setting up of a contract that would permit the handing over of the business on his death to Schiller, the proceeds going to the man's middle-aged widowed daughter. Okay so far, and perfectly legal, but Max was impatient and he did them both in. He did it so cleverly that they were not missed. The word was spread that they had retired together to a small cottage in Bavaria. Max took over the hotel."

Mark was becoming inured to shock. There had been so much revelation of evil in the last month that a little more ceased to be a surprise. "Could this crime be proved?"

"Yes. And Schwabl knows it. That is why he keeps the inner circle sweet."

"So. He could be stopped. Prosecuted. Your reluctance to shop him has always been your dependence on him?"

"Yes. That just about sums it up."

"I can see why you would be hesitant to stab him in the back. He pays your wages, and he would be merciless if he found you out, but why call me in on this?"

"Because I think you are still involved in ferreting for the truth of the Feldman affair, and I think the time has come go give you some reassurance. You will have supposed that there was a unity of intent in the Schiller organization, an unquestioning backing for Max Schwabl. I want to tell you that the truth is otherwise. Those of us who are in the know are now united in believing that we should line up on the side of justice. We are prime movers in a large international group that could repay the debt to the Feldman successors without too much difficulty. We believe that if Max Schwabl could be brought to justice in a regular way, the attending publicity would not condemn the company to an ignominious future. The Schiller entity would hiccup a little, and then carry on giving an honest service to travelers throughout its chain of hotels. In other words, we could do without him, and would welcome his departure."

"But you will not just go to the police here and tell them of the Saxony murders?"

"Not for the moment, no. The good reason for our reluctance is that Max is still at large. We are hoping now that his anxieties concerning the synagogue in London will lead him into problems from which he will not be able to extricate himself, and you should be the first to know that we have this belief. So long as we judge that we remain personally safe from a knife in the back — in other words, for so long as we can work together without him finding out, then we are on your side."

"What is he going to do in London, the synagogue documents?"

"Yes. But how he is doing to deal with it I do not know."

"He is able to get some help from questionable people in London though?"

"Yes. He has never fought shy of giving backhanders to villains here and there. He always knows where to knock on the door to get some help with seamy tasks."

Mark wondered whether to tell Gustav that the Jacobs had crossed the line between wickedness and honesty. He decided not to. That area of concern had not arisen in this conversation. Did Gustav know about the division of the wealth? He had not admitted so.

"So, anyway, I can feel free to call you if I think you could be helpful to us?"

"Yes. Any time."

Olga topped up the coffees. She said: "Mark, you must think that we are passing the buck rather, leaving you at the center of the problem and hoping that you will be able to achieve what has always been difficult for us. The fact is that Gustav has recognized honor in you, and that is an elusive quality in many people these days. We simply hope that assuring you of our support and being honest about it all will at least remove any fears you will have had about the threat of danger from here."

They lunched, amiably, and with plenty of small talk. Both his hosts were charming and Mark left Hamburg in the early evening happier than he had been when he arrived.

15

When Max Schwabl had landed at Heathrow, he took a taxi to his docklands hotel, indulged the usual careful VIP welcome and the attention that went with it, and dined. At eight- thirty, a man arrived in reception asking for him. Schwabl abandoned his crème broulet half eaten and went out to meet his visitor. There was no need for extravagant secrecy and a quiet corner of the hotel bar served as a briefing point. They spoke on familiar terms and Max gave his instructions. The man departed.

A few minutes after midnight, a van arrived close to the West London Synagogue and parked legally on a metered space within a few yards of the gutted building. One man got out and wandered casually to the front of the office building, examining it. He returned to the van and three more men joined him, carrying suitcases. Three went together up the steps. They chose their moment and ducked under the safety barriers. Within seconds, sure footed, and with the street lighting to help them at this stage, they disappeared into the fallen masonry and the mess of the fire. Hooded torches now enabled them to continue cautiously through the gutted reception area, and on into the connecting passage. The fourth man, acting as sentinel, strolled the adjacent street, the mobile phone in the palm of his hand connected to one that the intruders were carrying. They had attracted no attention. This was central London, with busy traffic on the nearby main street, and still many pedestrians, mostly the young for whom there are no limitations in pleasure hours.

The three boxes were easy to find. The suitcases were laid on the floor, opened, and emptied of the bundles of newspapers they contained. The string-secured boxes were then opened, and their contents packed gently into the cases. The newspapers were packed into the boxes, some of them with multiple folds to increase their bulk, and the boxes secured again. Care was taken to knot and bow the strings as they had been found. Before the final one was closed a small square of unexposed camera film, half the size of a postage stamp, was placed beneath its lid. If the lid remained down, the film would remain unexposed.

A brief check with the sentinel led to a short wait for the right moment of exit to arrive. Then the three carried their suitcases back to the van. Within half an hour the cases were on the floor of Max's suite in Docklands. A desk area had been prepared for the next task, passing each document, one side and then the other, beneath a tripod with a pre-focused digital camera mounted on it. One small spotlight sufficed to give each document adequate light for photographing. The process was tested, found good, and then the work began. It took nearly three hours. Max was careful to make sure that he saw each sheet of paper. Some he dealt with casually, and some he read carefully.

The documents were replaced in their original order in the suitcases. As the work neared completion, Max removed two envelopes from his briefcase, extracted papers from them and placed them in selected locations amongst the others. They were letters, careful forgeries produced in the styles and on the papers of another age. Careful thought and tactical intent had gone into them.

> The Uhland Manor House,
> Celle, Deutschland.
> May 5th, 1936
> The West London Synagogue,
>
> Dear Eli,
> I am pleased to learn, from your recent letter, that all the matters relating to the establishment of my trust with you have been satisfactorily

completed. I write now to tell you that I wish to add another beneficiary whom I intend should share equally in the eventual distribution of the estate.

As things stand, my principal heirs are my son, Johann Muller, and my grandson Gunther Muller, and, in the event of their deaths, their proved descendents. However, I have decided that it would be appropriate for me to include my other son, Heinrich Schwabl, currently a partner in Schwabl und Eppelsheimer, of Celle, for a half share. This young man was born of me with a lady of this district for whom I have had great affection over the years. Unfortunately, because of religious differences, I was unable to contemplate marrying her at the vital time. However, I was able to contribute to the bringing-up and education of our son. He has served me loyally on our estate here, and remains cherished. Please extend the terms of my bequest to include him fully, having a half share in the total with Johann. In the event of either one not living to benefit from the estate, the total accrues to the surviving other, or their descendents.

Yours very sincerely,
Kurt Feldman.
and the other

The Uhland Manor House,
Celle, Deutschland.
February 17th 1955.
The West London Synagogue,

Dear Mr.Jacobs,
Your kind letter of February 12th is to hand. The news contained therein has come as a great surprise as you may imagine. I knew, of course, that my father

had amassed great wealth during his lifetime. As you have accurately deduced, I was, unfortunately, an illegitimate offspring, and I had not expected that he would wish to include me in his intentions for the disposing of this estate. That he apparently did so is a great joy and comfort to me.

You mention that there were others who were to share in it. I had known, of course, of my half brother Johann, who, before he died tragically in the war, had assigned a half share in his hotels in the Munich area to me, including the *Freisinger Waldhaus*. We were very close as you may have gathered, and it was a great sadness to me that he was to suffer the same fate shared by so many others in those difficult times. Unhappily, I was not to know, because of the war, his son, who also died, and I believe he had children that I never had the pleasure of meeting.

I would not have wished for those heirs of Kurt Feldman to have escaped his generosity through tragedy, but I am grateful that he bore me in mind, and that I am, with your kind cooperation, to share some of his inheritance. I shall be in London shortly, and I place myself unreservedly in your hands, to discharge matters entirely as you recommend.

Yours very sincerely,
Heinrich Schwabl.

By five-thirty in the morning, the synagogue's precious papers had been restored to them, the three boxes apparently untouched. The piece of film negative was restored to a light proof container, returned to the hotel, and pronounced unexposed by the photographer. No one had been at the boxes. They would have needed a torch and the film would have been exposed.

Hal called Mark, "We were almost on the point of making a

disastrous mistake here. The boxes were not touched last night and I am now regarding that as extremely fortunate. I have taken them out of the passage, and they are now locked up again in the temple."

"Why the alarm then Hal?"

"We had been keeping all the papers relating to Feldman together, old and new. Now, if I had been in total control, I would have known that the new should be kept absolutely separate, but I have been using a lot of help as you can imagine, and missed out on an important priority. I have had one of our loyal and willing ladies in and she packed those boxes. Now, however, I have been looking for, and cannot find, a penciled note that I made reminding myself of the name of the hotel that Paul was staying at. Now that was a dangerous giveaway anyway, but more dangerous was my heading on the sheet, 'Feldman repayment. Mark meeting with Paul 2 pm.' I shall be going through the boxes shortly to recover it. When I have, do you want me to put the boxes out again Mark?"

If Hal was relieved, so was Mark. That could have been a disaster. "Yes please Hal. It is a long shot, but we may as well stick to the original plan. They may come tonight. We know that the boss is in town at the moment. Have you had any more contact with Paul or Alec?"

"Now that is a bit of a mystery Mark. Paul has checked out of his hotel and Alec is not contactable at his home. Odd really, because we still employ him, and he has not been anywhere near here."

This is worrying, thought Mark. They ended their conversation.

When Helga arrived back in Halle, to see Lise and Helmut before she went back to Stuttgart, their get together was more of a trance than a celebration. They were overwhelmed with the size of the check, and the realization that this represented just the start of a repayment process that would lead to the periodic arrival of similar amounts, left them in confusion. Joy? Yes, of course. But also indecision. These three honest people found it difficult to contemplate a changed life. For Lise, the thought that she could now, if she wished, change her lifestyle completely, was hard to come to terms with. This small terraced home had been their treasure for many years, and, as she looked around it, she wondered whether a transition into luxury would actually make life more comfortable.

The immediate benefit, gratefully understood and experienced, was the simple joy of having enough. No longer would Helmut have to sit at the end of each month and work out where their modest earnings would have to go. No longer would they have to worry about whether they could afford new curtains for a bedroom. No longer would they be concerned about the level of their insurance cover on the house and its contents. This conferred great solace on them.

The target for the benefits of the wealth would be their children and grandchildren. That was agreed. All three knew that the biggest joys of prosperity would not be their own self-indulgence, but would be the pleasure of bringing comfort to their descendents.

For Helmut, the prospect of retirement was nice. He had understood very well the reason for the cautions imposed on him by Mark, but he expected that the dust would settle eventually, and that he would be able to take life easier. For someone like him, who had led a long life submerged in hard work, with scant privilege, this thought was pleasant.

They all agreed that there was an important outstanding duty to perform now, before they went into detailed planning about the spread of the money, and that was to consult the Woodfords about a funeral for Gunther, and go over to England to offer their respect to this long-gone father. Helmut's telephone call to ask that this should be set up reached Sue. She dealt with it immediately. It was not complicated. There was no list of two hundred guests, no need for the preparation of obituaries, no large reception. There would only be a small group at the Church, the three Germans, the Woodfords, John Shaw and his wife, and Mark's mother. The date was fixed, just two days on, and she rang back to confirm it. The Helmanns would be met at London Airport and would stay with Mark's mother.

Mark, privy to all this, but taking some time out to pursue come necessary college business, would have been reluctant to allow the setting up these arrangements two days earlier, but he felt now that the only threat to them was Max Schwabl himself. They were all consoled by the reduction in pressure resulting from his lunch in Celle with the Richters.

Paul Jacobs' property in West Virginia had fulfilled a dream for him, and he was going to be able to keep it. It was nearly fifteen acres of mostly wooded land running down to a quiet riverside. At its center was a comfortable bungalow, verandad in the local style. One of its charms was its isolation, three miles from the nearest settlement, reached by a quiet road. Originally it had been a tobacco plantation. Paul was relaxing in his lounge in the early evening, easing himself out of jet lag resulting from his return from London yesterday. He felt happier now than he had done a week ago. The settlement had suited him, and pleased everyone else concerned.

He could return to the normality of his life here, mixing with friends locally, and indulging his favorite pastime, settling down with a good book. He had plans now to reconnect himself more to the Jewish community. He had stayed distant from this involvement as his conscience had begun to bother him more with his advancing age. The recent reconciliation with the synagogue in London has eased his mind. Yes, he was an old man now, but he no longer carried the burden of guilt to the same extent as in the past fifty years.

A bourbon and soda, well iced, as at his elbow. Being at the back of the house here, he had not heard a vehicle approaching along his graveled road, but the chimes of his doorbell were unmistakable. Callers were not unusual, often boaters coming up from the river looking for fresh water, or wanting local information in this remote area. He made his leisurely way to the hall.

The man on the step was unknown to him, but the accent in which he delivered his enquiry filled him with instant dread. "Mr. Jacobs?"

"Yes." The guttural utterance of the question made the declaration that followed unnecessary. Paul knew who it was.

"I am Max Schwabl."

"Oh."

"I have come to talk to you. May I come in?" He did not wait for an invitation, but was already half way through the door before his request had been completed. He looked around him with curiosity, seeing the layout of the house, and led the way through to the lounge. He saw the cocktail glass on the table by the sliding doors, and sat himself in the adjacent chair.

Paul followed, uncertain, unprepared, feeling resent but unable to express it. He stood. "What can I do for you? Why are you here?"

"I am here because we share a problem."

"We do?"

"Of course we do. You are well aware." He picked up the glass and sniffed at it. "I think one of these would suit me very well Mr. Jacobs, if you would oblige. It has been a long journey to get here."

Paul went to the drinks cabinet by the wall. While he was pouring, Schwabl said: "You have no servants to do your bidding Mr. Jacobs?"

"Not at this time of the day. I have some help in the mornings, inside and out, but I like privacy in the afternoons."

Schwabl nodded. "This problem Mr. Jacobs. You rang me at Celle not many days ago, to warn me of interference, someone meddling. So, we have never met, but each of us had been protective towards the other, and we have had occasional contact. It is now fifty years since you and my father consorted to make yourselves wealthy. You were employed by the West London Synagogue as their office manager, and my father arrived to claim an estate that had been left in trust with you by a man called Kurt Feldman. You, it seems, shared his hope of a better life, and you contrived, between you, to claim that estate and share it. You now, as I see, live comfortably as a result, and I, benefiting from my father's initiative, preside over a successful hotel business based in Germany. His money contributed much to the early years of that business."

Paul sat. He was puzzled, his mind thrusting through the recent events in England, trying to identify a vulnerable element that might have led to this encounter. He could not yet do so. He waited.

Schwabl went on: "Do you know anything about recent happenings at the synagogue over there? Did you know that earlier this year a *Luftwaffe* pilot was dug up in England, and he was carrying letters apparently that reawakened interest in the 1956 claim of the Feldman estate?"

Paul had to lie. He was a bad liar, but he had to try. He was scared now. He wondered if it would be noticed. "No, Herr Schwabl, I have heard nothing of that. Tell me about it. It could be worrying for us."

If Schwabl doubted the genuineness of this answer he did not show it yet. "We know, you and I, that the conversion of the estate for our joint profit was fraud, to put it simply. You, of course, were personally involved, but I was not. However, I am my father's son, and because I did not try to alter things when he passed away, I sit here bearing as much guilt as you do. Tell me Mr. Jacobs — do you feel guilty?"

"I never have. No. Your father and I agreed at the time that the money was going to waste sitting in a trust that benefited nobody. At least we have put it to good use. Your share evidently went to a good business cause as you are telling me. Mine has been harmlessly used." He waved an arm across the panorama facing them through the wide doorway.

"Well, harmlessly used or not, I can tell you that it is now at risk. I have been able to provide certain protections for myself against anyone claiming the money back from me, but I have been worrying about you. I have reasoned that, if certain people thought they would have a go at me, then they would consider you as a target also. You have had no approach from anyone, an Englishman, anyone from Germany?"

"No."

Schwabl looked at Jacobs closely. He did not want to turn his cowering fear into incoherence yet. Time enough. He had more to learn. He sat back.

"I lead a quiet life here Herr Schwabl. I have very little contact with England any more, and no one knows where I am. I am now an American citizen. My intention when I came here was to keep out of the way of any probing that might start at the synagogue, and I have been successful in that. I can understand that you would be concerned if people started taking an interest in where the money went, but I would not be their first point of enquiry I think."

He went on, beads of perspiration how showing on his brow. "Anyway, we always knew that it would be very hard for anyone to prove what we did, your father and I. While I was in London I was able to keep all the records under my control, and he, for his part, assured me that there was no one alive in Germany who could interfere with what we did. They were all dead, most of them killed in the war."

Schwabl rose, and gazed out onto the tidy lawns, sipping his drink. He turned back to Paul. "What about your son, Alec. Where is he?"

"He is in London."

"He works at the synagogue still?"

"Yes. We thought it prudent to leave him there as a protection."

"He is there now?"

"Yes."

"No. He is not."

"Pardon?"

Schwabl raised his voice, leaning towards Paul for emphasis, his heavy lips moist with saliva. "He is missing. Missing, you understand? We heard that yesterday. Why is he missing? I had one of my staff in London call the synagogue and ask for him. They said he was not there. And they said that they could not take a message because they did not know if and when he would be about again."

"I did not know that he was missing."

"Why does a man go missing from anywhere Mr. Jacobs? Fear Mr. Jacobs. Your son has made himself scarce because something at the synagogue has driven him away. Things are happening there that I want to know about. There is danger there for me anyway, and to hell with you. Where is he?"

"I don't know. Why did you ask your man in London to call and try to find him?"

"Because we have someone there who keeps us informed, but cannot tell us everything."

Fear now dominated Paul's mind. Loyalties were becoming dilute.

Good intentions were softening into self-preservation. He nodded slowly, saying nothing, but allowing his submission to become evident.

"I think you are deceiving me Mr. Jacobs. I have more than a suspicion that you are consorting with the enemy. I think that somehow you have preserved your freedom, but you have done so by leaving me at risk. I think it likely that you have blown the whistle on me, or you are about to do so, so that I may find myself in a very exposed position, and will have to pay a heavy price. This will not only be in money possibly, but also in prestige and reputation. I run a hotel business and I have no intention of allowing it to suffer because of something unimportant that happened years ago. You have been talking to them have you not? Answer me." He leant close to Paul.

Paul remained silent. Schwabl went on: "You have knowledge that could ruin me. Perhaps you have already parted with some of it. So far, down the years, you have kept your side of the bargain that you made with my father, but you are a big risk to me now, and I have to protect myself. What did you do?"

"I have agreed to repay most of the money to the people who are entitled to it."

"The two sisters from Halle?"

"Yes, I think so."

"And are they expecting to get some from me as well?"

"I don't know."

"Have I come up in any discussions?"

"Yes," said Paul slowly.

"Tell me about them."

"I think they are hoping that they could persuade you to make some repayment as well."

"On what grounds. What information do they have to give them some hope that I could be made to agree? All the original documentation at the time of the share out had your signature on it, not my father's."

Paul shrugged. "They know that your father killed the Mullers at the *Freisinger Waldhaus.*"

It was Schwabl's turn to show shock. "They know that?"

"Yes. And they know that your father worked for Feldman at the *Uhland* estate, and went to *Freisinger* early in the war to claim it, and the other hotels that the Mullers owned. When the Mullers did not claim *Uhland* because of fear of being exposed as having a Jewish connection during the war, he claimed that as well."

"How do you think they intend to use this knowledge?"

Paul shook his lowered head. "I have no idea. I have not been close to all their discussions. I simply agreed, when they asked me, to repay most of the money. That has not been a difficult thing for me to go along with."

"So — I am to take comfort in the fact that, evidently, they have not given all this information to the police in your case, leading to troubles with them, and that, probably, if I paid them the money, I would be left in peace in the same way?"

"I think that would be the case, yes."

"They have not threatened you with the police?"

"No. They have been kept out of it."

"Did you know that they had a bad fire at the West London Synagogue recently?"

"Yes."

"Did you know, or did they know, that I caused it — my people in London?"

"Yes. They know that."

"Well. Be that as it may Mr. Jacobs, let me tell you that I am not going to give a penny to anyone. I am not going to be dictated to. And let me tell you something else. By allying yourself to these people you have become cornered. Your loyalties now are going to be confused, and therefore dangerous. Did it not occur to you that we should have stayed together in this thing, keeping our common interest, preserving our secret? Was it not obvious to you when they were targeting you for some sort of admission guilt, that whatever you agreed to would implicate me as well? Did it not? And what help can I expect from you, now that you have gone this far with them?"

Paul's abject fear in the face of this tirade moderated to allow some aggression to appear, a defensive instinct. He stood up, facing Schwabl, raising his voice that had been timid hereto. "All I have done is agreed to repay some money. Nothing more. No disclosures. No involvement of you. And what damage do you think I could do to you, even now, that did not dig me in deeper myself. If you are determined not to take a share in the responsibility for your father's actions, and if you are so convinced that they could not get at you because it was his crime and not yours, then why are you here? Nothing to fear is nothing to fear. Precisely how do you think I remain a threat?"

Schwabl leaned close to him, glowering. Paul could feel the spittle ejected from his fleshy mouth amongst the powerful shouts. "Because you are the only living person who knows the whole truth. Because you have demonstrated that you are prepared to part with that truth. And because your disclosures implicate me."

The last ten words of this tirade were softened by its deliverer. They were being interrupted. Paul was relieved. There were shouts coming from the direction of the river bank, echoing through the trees and clear through the open doorway.

Max asked Paul: "What's going on?"

"Boaters. There is a quay down there where they can draw water. I often hear them at this time of the year. Sometimes they moor there overnight. I have never minded if they walk up through my ground to the road. They sometimes call a taxi and go into town for a meal and a cocktail. That sort of thing."

Max stepped out onto the paved front of the house. Two couples, early middle-aged perhaps, were walking towards them. The leader waved, and greeted Paul, advancing with an outstretched hand. 'Hi. We're here for a while. Is that okay? We are going to find something to eat. How's things with you?"

"Fine," said Paul. It was easier to find a smile than it had been thirty seconds ago. The party walked on round the house and it became quiet again. Max, apparently ignoring Paul, walked on down towards the water, hands in pockets. Paul followed. He knew he had to. He knew that if he lingered he would be summoned. He was not going to given the chance to use the telephone, or jump in his car and make a break for it.

Max stood on the jetty and took in the view. In front of him was a small cabin cruiser, perhaps forty feet long. It had cabins fore and aft, and a central well where he could see the steering wheel and the engine housing. Forward, there was a deck area with a flush hatch, obviously a chain locker used for rope and fender storage. He looked round him. Left and right the otherwise deserted river disappeared into the panorama of tree lined banks. He turned to face the house again. No one about. Without any warning he grabbed Paul, spun him round, put an arm round his throat, and laid him out on the wooden planking of the jetty. Within reach was the slack tail end of a mooring rope. He wound it round Paul's neck, and stood again, putting a foot on his victim's head. He hauled viciously on both end of the rope in his hands. Within one minute Paul was dead.

Max, looked around him again, and then stepped onto the cruiser. He lifted the hatch cover on its hinges. In another thirty seconds he had gone swiftly though Paul's pockets to remove any identification, and the job had been done. The limp body of Paul Jacobs lay amongst the sailor's oddments.

Max walked slowly back in the direction of the house. It had been a good thing to do. The threat of interference by this man was now removed. Strangulation with rope had been prudent. No fingerprints. He knew that the locker would be untouched for days at a time. The body would be found? Yes, of course, but not for some time hopefully. The cause of death would be difficult to establish, and what remained of him would be miles away before long. He had lived a quiet life here evidently, and would not be quickly missed.

He wandered casually back into the house and finished his drink. Through to Paul's office area then, and a quick browse. Anything interesting? Not much, and he was not greatly bothered. He hit the road again for the drive back to Philadelphia. He was watchful as he left the Jacob's ground. Anyone about? No. Deserted.

He was back at the airport much earlier than he had expected, and managed to get on an earlier flight. He had expected that he might be here overnight. The amiable girl at the check-in asked him if his visit to America had been a happy one. He nodded. Yes thank you. Mission completed.

Alec rang his father from London. This was nothing more than a courtesy. How did your journey go? There was no reply, and this puzzled him because the call had been arranged. He left a voice mail. He tried the mobile also, but there was no reply there either. It was switched off. No great anxiety for a while, after all, father may have been out for good reasons. He was free to come and go. However, as the evening wore on he did begin to worry. He called a known friend of his father's in the local community and explained his puzzlement. The man said he would go out to the house. Because of the time difference it was six in London, but one in West Virginia.

Two hours later he called Alec from his father's house. He told him that he had tried the door bell, got no reply, so he went round the front to find that the big doors were open. No one about, but there were two glasses on the coffee table by the doors that still smelled of liquor.

Alec asked if the friend knew of any visitors to father recently. No. They agreed that the police should be called. Alec rang off, puzzled and not a little worried. He thought of Celle. What else? He rang Mark.

"It's Alec. I have been trying to get Father on the 'phone in America. He went back yesterday. The timing of the call had been arranged before he went, but I could get no reply. A friend of his has just been out to the house, and has found signs that someone was visiting because there were two glasses on the coffee table. But no sign of Father. Also, although there was no evidence of a forced break in, there was something of a mess in his office, papers strewn about. I have told his friend over there to call the police. Something nasty may have happened. Is it Celle?"

"If he had popped out on some innocent errand, and forgotten you were to ring him, would he have left the house open?"

"No. Absolutely not. And an innocent errand would have been local and quick. He has been missing now for more than twelve hours. What else can I do? Do you have any ideas?"

"We have not known where you are Alec. Are you still in London?"

"Yes, but not at home while it's risky."

"Okay." To Mark there was only one explanation. Schwabl. Alec would have to face it. He told him so. "Let's hope that they can make sense of it over there Alec. We are too far away to do much. The finger points at Schwabl of course, and I have good reason to doubt whether anyone else at Celle is involved. I wonder if Max is over there, or if he set someone up to do something nasty for him. We cannot know for the moment. Can you give me a return 'phone number? If I learn anything I will get straight to you. And I am also going to ask you to trust me with the number of your father's friend in America." He scribbled the numbers down and rang off. There was not much else he could do beyond being sympathetic.

He rang Gustav. They had a brief exchange of greetings. Mark said: "I have just found out that Paul Jacobs has disappeared from his home in America, and there is evidence that some violence had taken place there. Tell me Gustav, is Max back with you from his London trip, or could he be across the Atlantic?"

"Mark. I do not know, but I can probably find out. It would be normal for him, as for all of us in the company, to charge a flight to the company account, rather than a personal one. Give me a few minutes so that I can go into our bank on line, and I may have a clue. I shall then have to trace back to the payee details, airline or whatever, and query any travel times with them."

Mark waited with bated breath for the reply. It did not take long.

"Yes. He flew out of London Airport to Philadelphia last night, and is booked back again today on the ten thirty flight from there to London. Is that helpful? Do we think that something terrible has happened?"

"It seems likely. I am still uncertain. I will let you know when I have something to pass on."

He rang the number in America. It was now almost nine in the evening. It would be four over there. The 'phone was answered instantly. "Who am I talking to?" asked Mark.

"John Levine. Who am I talking to?"

Good evening John. My name is Mark Woodford. I am speaking to you from England. I am a friend of Alec and Paul Jacobs, and I am talking to you with Alec's consent. He gave me your number just a few minutes ago. Have you talked to the police?"

"Yes. You know of the problem at Paul's house then?"

"Yes. But we have reason to think that it may be a bigger problem than you suppose. I cannot go into details for the moment, but I can tell you that the Jacobs father and son do have a complication in their lives dating back many years. This relates to a financial matter in which Paul was involved with a German company. We know that there have been some disputes lately concerning this, and we know that feeling have run high. We think it very likely that Paul has been got at in someway. His life may have been at risk."

"My purpose in ringing you is to ask you to give some important information to your police immediately. If they can trace a Max Schwabl who is about to fly out of Philadelphia to Amsterdam, they will be able to check his movements back. If we knew for certain that he had been there it would be helpful. This man heads a large hotel group in Germany called the Schiller Corporation. We do not know if there were other people involved, or if there was a car hire or whatever, but this man had the motive to damage Jacobs. Philadelphia is not far from West Virginia, and would be a good choice to travel to and from. I have just had confirmation of his presence in your general area from his company's office in Germany."

The man laboriously took all this down. They had to be careful with the exact spelling of Schwabl. Mark told him that he suspected he would not be able to help the police directly, because protocol would probably make it necessary for them to proceed via the British police, but, even so, he would be available to answer any questions, and he gave him his home 'phone number.

What now? Tenterhooks. Mark rang Alec and told him what had

happened. He was saddened at the prospect of a dead father. They suggested he talk to Hal who would give him more comfort than any one else.

It was wait and see time again. Sue said: "I wonder where Schwabl is at this moment? I wonder if they will catch him? What a lot of problems that would solve. What a relief that would be for us. You particularly. You seem to have been caught up in this for ever."

Mark sighed. "Yes. Calculus is easier."

16

It was Saturday, the funeral day. Mark was about early and went to pick up the Bormanns at the airport. They were a cheerful group. The fact that this was a time to honor their dead father did not impair their determination to enjoy what was, for all of them, an exciting adventure. This was not going to be a funeral in the normal way. This was not the lament of a family over a recent death. It was to be a genuine gesture of remorse, but time had healed the wound. Also, they wanted to share the joy that had come into their lives with the newly arriving wealth.

Mark took them his mother's. They were to meet John and his wife at the church later, and then return to the big house for a dinner. Mother was full of the arrangements for it, the first time a large group had sat round the big Victorian table in her dining room since the days when she and her diplomat husband frequently hosted foreign dignitaries.

Mark was to go home for Sue, preoccupied with looking nice for the service and the dinner after. She told him that there had been a call for him from America. She knew that he was due back imminently, and said that he would call. It was John Levine.

"Mark. I am glad to have caught you. We have to be careful here to work out the time difference before we bother people on your side of the Atlantic."

"No problem. How are things working out over there?"

"I have worries that you should know about. As you can imagine, yesterday was something of a shock. We cannot be absolutely certain that Paul was murdered because there is no body yet, and there were no witnesses, but everything points to that conclusion. The sudden loss of a friend through violence is not an easy thing to come to terms with. But I have been following things up."

" When we talked yesterday there was only one topic, and that was the urgent matter of getting your information to the police here. I did that immediately, and we now learn that they did follow it up. However, they tell me this morning that this Schwabl man was not intercepted at either end of his flight to London. He caught an earlier flight from Philadelphia than he had originally booked, and had arrived in London and disappeared before the alert to intercept him had been put in place. Just one of those things."

Mark said: "So. He is now in London somewhere, and if there is a police alert to catch him, he will not be able to go much further will he?"

"No. I imagine not. They will watch all your exits — airports and ferries. I wonder if he actually knows that they are after him? He will have left here assuming that he was in the clear. What is certain now is that he was actually here. He left his fingerprints all over the place. They are known to be his because they match others recovered from the car he hired, and he contracted that in his own name. He obviously thought that he was not going to be connected with this business, and was going to be off and gone before there was any alarm. Your call to me to get things going was timely."

"Any sign of Paul Jacobs yet?"

"No. Not that we know of. Our conclusion remains that he was murdered. At the outset, the police had reservations about that, but once I had explained to them about the old dispute between Paul and Schwabl, they have accepted that there could have been violence or worse. Not finding a body is the problem. He could have been dumped anywhere between here and the Airport. We shall have to wait and see, but meanwhile I have something else to mention to you, and that is something that I have not mentioned to the police. You told me yesterday that Paul had some old problems. Well, there were several of us amongst his friends here that knew about them."

"We knew, because he told us, something about the benefit that he gained from an unclaimed estate in London in the fifties. We knew that he was going to make some restitution. I also knew that he kept with him some documentation that related to the estate, and his part in dealing with it. I went up there last night to have a search about, in case the man who did him in had come to look for it and taken it away. Well, he didn't. There is a file there that I have looked at briefly, and, although I do not understand all the implications of its contents, it is clearly legally important. Apart from anything else there are letters from a Heinrich Schwabl in which he threatens Paul to arrange this and that in no uncertain language. My conclusion is that this is not a matter of concern to our police. It relates to things in Paul's life that were Europe based, and you made me aware that you were in the know about them."

Mark said: "This is interesting. It is valuable information. It makes sense that he should have kept it close to himself. I am surprised not to have known about it before, because he and I were together not many days ago, talking openly about his involvement with the estate, and neither he nor his son mentioned having this reserve of information. His intention, obviously, was to keep them as a protection. In which case it did not work did it?"

"No. It did not. Do you have any suggestions? I can give them to the police here, but I do not feel obliged to do so. Would you like them sent on to you?"

"Mr. Levine, I am going to make a suggestion. The man most concerned with this in England is Rabbi Hal Reznikov of the West London Synagogue. I am going to see if I can find him now and ask him to give you a ring. Although I have been involved in the business of trying to determine what went wrong with the settlement of that estate all those years ago, I do not act with any official authority. My guess is that he will ask you to mail them across to him, but I would prefer that he request that, and he will be able to tell you of some of his wider concerns."

Mark found Hal. It was the Jewish Sabbath and he was busy at the synagogue.

"Hal. Bad news. We cannot be absolutely certain yet, but we think the Paul Jacobs was killed yesterday, at his place in America, and the finger points at Max Schwabl. We know he was out there, and he had the motive of course."

There was hesitation while this gentle man absorbed the news. "Is there no end to this ghastly business Mark? What next? How do they know it was Schwabl?"

"Circumstantial evidence for the most part. They know he was at the house. It would be more definite if they had a body, but they don't yet. Schwabl is back in London now we think. Anyway, he is being sought by the police now for certain, and it will serve us well if they catch him." Mark went on to tell Hal of his conversation on moments ago with John Levine. He passed on the number.

Hal had more to say. "We think that the papers in the boxes were interfered with. We recovered them from the passage last night, and I found that penciled note that worried us, but we also found as we unpacked it all that there were two letters in there that were not in the original set of documents. It is unlikely that we missed them when we were collating the material, so we think that they were certainly placed there somehow."

"What is their topic Hal? What did they say?"

"I have them here. Hang on and I will read them to you." He did.

As Mark listened it all became clear. "They were plants Hal. They absolutely absolve the elder Schwabl of any complicity in the fraud of 1956 if they are to be believed. They make it look as though the whole guilt lies with Jacobs, that Schwabl was drawn in by Jacobs. Lies Hal. Let me tell you that we happen to know that Max Schwabl was in London two nights ago, staying at his hotel in docklands. I think that he arranged for the boxes to be interfered with somehow, enabling those two forged letters to be put in amongst the other stuff. He probably gave himself an opportunity to look at the rest of it is my guess. And he will have seen your note about the Jacobs meeting with the Helmanns."

"So we are still in deep trouble, and I am making it worse leaving notes around."

"Not so Hal. We are getting out of trouble is the truth be known.

Schwabl is in trouble himself. We do know that he flew into London last night, and that there is a search going on for him that will prevent him flying on to Germany, or using a ferry. Three days ago I would have joined you in deep anxiety, but now I think we are paddling in safer waters. I do not think you are going to be a target for any sort of nastiness now."

Mark rang Gustav at home. "Just to update you. It is pretty certain that Max did for Paul Jacobs, and the American police believe that he did. They have his fingerprints from the Jacobs' house and also from the car he rented in his own name. No body yet, but everything is pointing to murder. They put out a net to catch him at Philadelphia and at London Airport, but he caught an earlier flight than the one you quoted to me, and he is loose in London."

Gustav was thoughtful. "Does he know he is being sought do we think?"

"Probably not if he got clear through before they raised the alarm."

"I wonder if they know anything else about him — the hotel connection?"

"Yes. They do. I gave that information to the friend of Jacobs in America who contacted the police there. They will already be targeting the docklands hotel I imagine. Perhaps they have him already."

"Can you check up? It would be nice to know."

"Not advisable Gustav. If they have caught him without my help, and he is to be brought to justice for the Jacobs business, then that closes the matter. It would be better if I remained uninvolved because of the dead man at the synagogue and a few other things."

After he put his 'phone down, Gustav called his wife through to their lounge. He told her of the Virginia events. "She said: "You realize of course that they will not arrest him for what they know so far. They may want to question him. 'We know that you were there. What can you tell us? Did you meet with Jacobs, or was he elsewhere? He is missing and you may have been the last person to have seen him.' If they have no body, then they are going to be hesitant about locking Max up. And because he is so quick thinking, he would certainly wriggle out."

"Yes."

"If they cannot be certain yet that he killed this man Jacobs, but they are on the watch for him to question him, then this would be a good time to tell them about the Saxony business. They would certainly want to put him behind bars for that, and the mere fact that he could be proved to have been wicked once, would harden their attitudes in seeking to prove a repeat."

Gustav heard her out and recognized the sense of her logic. He nodded, and picked up the 'phone again. Fifteen minutes later, he was sitting in the office of an acquaintance, a local inspector of detectives. They knew each other well, not as personal friends particularly, but as mutually respectful long-term residents of Celle..

"So. You have a worry Gustav?"

"Yes. I am about to surprise you Wilhelm. I am going to tell you something that you should have known about long ago, and the time has come for action to be taken. Only you, and the extended police network internationally, can deal with it now. If you ask your colleagues in Saxony to go back into their records they will find that there is an unsolved matter of two people, father and daughter, who mysteriously became missing seven years ago. I know they were murdered. They were the owners of the Oberland Hotel in Zeitz, near Leipzig. Seven years ago."

Wilhelm leant forward at his desk and reached for a pen. As a professional policeman, accustomed to life's indelicacies, he showed no surprise. He listened quietly. "Go on."

"Living out on the *Nordstrasse*, at an address I shall give you, is a retired secretary of the Schiller organization, Gerda Imhoff. She is now in her late sixties, and worked at *Uhland* well and loyally until her retirement about four years ago. This unfortunate woman was the former personal secretary to Max Schwabl. She witnessed that murder."

"She told no one?"

"Yes. Me. But she will have told no one else simply because of the intimidation of Max Schwabl. It will not have been apparent to you, or to most of the people who associate with him as employees, neighbors, or residents of our town, that he has a relentless streak in him. He is a clever man who generally gives the rest of the world an impression of calm and efficient business behavior, but I can tell you that he is also a man who, if he sees the need, gains his ends by punching people on the nose rather than reasoning with them. Gerda was threatened with a punch on the nose, and has remained quiet since, knowing that her bullying boss was still only a mile away, and could descend on her wrathfully at any time."

"You are going to tell me that Schwabl also had his fist poised ready to have a go at you?"

"Yes. On that matter and on a number of others where he has stepped out of line."

"Why choose now to tell us this?"

"Because it is likely that Max Schwabl has been involved in the violent intimidation, or worse, of a Jew living in West Virginia. He has had a connection with this man going back many years. His father Heinrich, whom you will remember well, was a partner with the Jew in the fraudulent claiming of an estate in London in 1956. It has also become possible now to prove the involvement of Max Schwabl and his father in that crime."

Wilhelm stood, and walked to his window. "Are you able to consolidate what you are telling me with more detail?"

"Yes. I think so. I just about have chapter and verse. There has been much happening lately, particularly in England, that has alarmed those of us at *Uhland* who have some knowledge of the Schwabl wickedness. I have become unavoidably involved, and it is time it was stopped. You will want to check out the facts, but my expectation is that you will initiate a search for Schwabl based on the Saxony murder, and that will lead on to his being questioned about crimes elsewhere."

The computer at the corner table was set to record voice, and Gustav told the whole story. As he was doing so, he realized that it would take some time for an arrest search to be set in motion. The police would want to talk to Gerda first, and consult with their offices elsewhere. He just hoped that Max would not be able to do much more damage before the law caught up with him.

They had not caught Max Schwabl yet. He had flown into London, arriving at five thirty that morning, and had taken a taxi to his hotel, jubilant at the success of his American excursion, and quite unaware that he had stirred up a hornet's nest behind him. He was lavishly welcomed as usual, and his cases were taken up to the penthouse suite. He followed them up called for a coffee, showered, and then went to bed to recover from the privations of the flight, and the stress of jet lag. He awoke at eleven feeling ready to take on the world again.

He called Gustav, now back home, on the bedside 'phone. "I am back in London. Anything I should know about?"

Gustav had been expecting a call. He had made up his mind to continue to play the part of the loyal aide. It would make little difference to the outcome.

"Yes Max. I am glad you have called. We have a serious and immediate problem."

"Which is?"

"The police in West Virginia say that they suspect you killed Paul Jacobs yesterday. They have no body yet, but they do believe there was a death. Perhaps you didn't do it?"

"I did do it. How do they know?"

"They got your fingerprints from the car you rented, all over the wheel and elsewhere. Matching prints were found at the Jacobs house, on a glass and in an office area there."

"How do you know about this?"

""Woodford told me last night."

"Well. How the hell did he know?"

"I don't know the details, but evidently someone over there passed the information to him, and he wanted to warn us. I am sure his intentions were good. Anyway Max, you have a problem."

"What I cannot understand is how. I was utterly careful. There were some people about on the river there, but they were well out of the way when I did the deed. And I disposed of him in a quiet place — not a soul in sight. Hell!"

"If they are looking for you Max, it will only be a matter of time before they link you to the hotel. That is a dangerous place for you to be."

"Have they made any approach to you yet?"

"No. Nothing yet. What can we do? You will not be able to go through any airports there now. Any passport control will find you. Are we worrying unnecessarily? Is there any way that they could prove that you did the thing, suspicion or not?"

Max stood up from the edge of the bed, naked, frustrated, vengeful, but realistic. "Probably. The fingerprints will have given them all they need."

"The trouble is, you will not be able to claim that you were elsewhere. Air travel reservations are conclusive proof of presence."

"Yes. Well. I have to get out of here anyway. Stand by over there Gustav, either in the office or at home. I may need some help from you, and I shall want to know where you are." They left it at that.

Gustav, putting the 'phone down slowly, pondered. He knew that Max was in deep trouble. Even if he managed to get back to Celle, he would be had for the Saxony affair if nothing else. He was finished one way or the other. The Schiller Group would be doing without him. Go to London quietly? Find Woodford? Be in on the final chapter of this terrible business, or linger here quietly, impotent, and frustrated? At least over there he could possibly help to drive the knife in finally. Woodford had command, and near him was the best place to be.

Five hundred miles away, Max rang reception and asked them to send Richard, his head chef, up to the penthouse suite. This man arrived moments later in his whites. Max said to him: "I am in a bit of trouble Richard. It all leads on from the synagogue raid you organized for me last week. I have just come back from America where I have straightened out a long-standing dispute, and the police may be on my tail. They don't have anything positive to work on because I cleared up behind me, but they do know I was there. Do me another of your favors. I need a false passport. Get one organized. Once I am back in Germany I can get organized and put this all behind me, but here I am vulnerable."

Richard nodded. "Okay Max. I shall need your current German passport and about two days to get it done. Will you be here?"

"No. It's dangerous. I shall go and stay at the Carpenters Arms, and then I shall know that I have some good help if I need it. Give Garry a ring and tell him I am on my way. Tell him I shall want to borrow a reliable car, and keep your mobile switched on in case I need you. Also, tell Garry I will want to borrow an automatic. Six-shot, and a couple of spare magazines. I do not expect to have to rub anyone out this trip, but the loud noise and some splintered woodwork normally gets good results."

"Okay. What will you be doing for the time being?"

"Not long ago, I authorized the payment of a large sum of money to an interfering English bastard who has been dogging my steps and getting in the way. One of my problems while I am here is going to be getting at money. Once I am home, no problem, but here they may keep a watch on cash point withdrawals or something. I could draw some funds from here of course, but the better route, as I see it, would be to go and take my money back from this dangerous swine in Buckinghamshire. He has not earned the money, and I need it."

"You know where to go?"

"Max patted his briefcase on the bedroom table. "Yes. Some time ago he gave Gustav the address of the house close to which the body of a *Luftwaffe* pilot had been found. I expect to find him there. If he is not at home then I will wait for him, or ask you to get involved in tracing him. We shall see. But I will locate him, believe me."

17

The funeral had been a warm affair. A very quiet church and no frills. No one would be attending the cremation, but the Woodfords were to pick up the ashes and take them across to Germany on a visit to the Bormanns at Christmas. Meanwhile, the Germans were enjoying the hospitality of Mark's mother. After the service the ladies, including John's wife, went together to look at the local town. Mother had some more bits to find for the meal this evening, and they would tour the shops and sights. The men were to go back to the big house. Helmut was anxious to see the spot where Gunther had been found. John backed his car in at the side of the house. First priority was to brew a pot of tea and sit with it in the kitchen.

Helmut, armed with his camera, walked with John along the ridge to find the hallowed spot. Muffin went along as guide. Mark stood by at the phone. His mother would be calling him when they were ready to come back from town, and he would go in to pick them up.

There was a knock on the front door. Mark walked through to open it. A large man stood there, reddish haired, hands on hips, dressed in a city suit which was a little out of place here.

"Mr. Woodford?"

Mark knew instantly who it was. There was no mistaking the guttural pronunciation.

"Yes. Max Schwabl?"

"Who else Mr. Woodford. I am here to talk to you." He moved forward, climbing the stone steps, and pushed Mark backwards with a firm push of a palm on his chest. He slammed the door behind him. The intruder looked around him, seeing the open doors to the library and the lounge, and glancing along the passage that led to the back of the house. He turned to face Mark again.

"We have unfinished business Mr. Woodford. The unfinished business is the money I wasted, giving it to you to keep your mouth shut. You have not kept your mouth shut. You have blown your mouth around so widely that I am now in trouble. All because of you..."

Mark intervened: "I think you must have misunderstood what has been happening Herr Schwabl. I have been on your side. How have you come to suppose otherwise?" Mark knew to this was not going to be the moment to act the rebel. He had to soften this man's attitude, and that would only happen if he was conciliatory.

"I don't believe you Mr. Woodford. Whenever I talk to anyone about what has been happening lately concerning my father's visit to London in 1956, your name comes up. You are getting in the way Mr. Woodford." He raised a hand again to push at Mark's chest.

"I have come here for something Mr. Woodford. My money. We gave you all that money to keep quiet, and all that has happened is that you have made more noise. More noise Mr. Woodford!. I want that money back. We are going to get it. Now! You are going to get your car and we are going to go to draw as much out of your bank as they have available in their till. And you are going to transfer the rest that you owe me to my account in Germany. Do you understand Mr Woodford? His voice had risen as he went.

"And if I refuse Herr Schwabl?"

Max put his hand in the right pocket of his jacket, and produced the automatic, gray, shining, and menacing, his index finger poking through the guard, and white on the trigger.

"There will be no arguments Mr. Woodford. We will do as I say. Let me tell you why you will agree with me. Because this will not be aimed at you Mr. Woodford. It will be aimed at your wife. I will take her out Mr. Woodford if you do not do as I tell you."

There was the sound of an engine and the crunch of wheels on the gravel in the drive. Max stepped back, his expression still menacing, still facing Mark, gun still leveled. He turned half sideways and opened the front door. The car had turned in the large forecourt and a man was getting out, Gustav Richter. Max exclaimed and moved out into the open.

"Gustav? Gustav. What the hell are you doing here? You should be at Celle. That's where I told you to stay. And why here?" Then the realization dawned on him. Traitor! "So — Gustav, you are stabbing me in the back. You are consorting with this bastard." He waved the gun in the direction of Mark on the top step, and then his voice rose to become a savage shout. "Bastards, all of you...." He ran down the steps and raised his gun towards Gustav. Mark, on his blind side now, ran down after him and charged him in the back, just as he fired two shots. Defensively, his target had backed off in the face of the gun and was not hit. Max followed him, moving out onto the open gravel, his gun raised again. Gustav was now ducked behind the trunk of the car.

John and Helmut were returning along the ridge and had almost reached the garden when they heard the shots. John led the way to the rescue, running to the corner of the house, and looking cautiously round its edge. He saw Max in the middle of the drive, gun raised. In an instant he was into his car beside him, key in, and, at the second when the still warm engine fired, he turned the corner and headed straight for Max. The gun was swung round and leveled at the wind screen. Too late Max. John lowered his head, thrust his throttle foot down, and hit Max at knee level, sending him sprawling. John stamped on the brakes and the car skidded to a halt.

Instantly, Helmut was round the front of John's car and put his foot firmly on Max's gun hand. The weapon fell loose. Helmut kicked it away a yard to his left, stepped back and reached down for it. One big step took him back to Max, in agony from broken leg bones, his face a contorted grimace of pain. Helmut put two shots into his head a point blank range.

John, still in his car, backed it away and stopped the engine. Sudden silence. Muffin, alarmed by the sound of the shots, had made himself scarce, but now reappeared, putting his nose into Mark's hand for consolation. Gustav walked slowly across to join the stationary group of three — Helmut with the gun dangling downwards in his hand, John looking down at the motionless Max, and Mark anxiously looking down the drive, fearful of the shots having been heard.

Mark looked at Gustav. "Unexpected Gustav, but welcome."

Gustav nodded. "Thanks Mark. I knew I should come and see you, but I didn't expect to walk into this."

Helmut dropped the gun onto the gravel. They were all silent for a long moment.

Mark said:" Well. Police I suppose," half turning to go back into the house.

John stepped sideways to stop him, two palms raised. "Hang on Mark. Think about it a moment." He pointed at Max. "This man deserved what has happened to him. Perhaps it is not the conventional way for justice to be done, but we all know he was evil, and he was going to get his just deserts before long. All that has happened here is that we have taken a short cut."

The three men turned towards him. He was emphatic. "We can keep quiet about this. We have to put it all behind us and pretend that it didn't happen. The ladies have no need to know. They will be back here shortly and we have a merry dinner to enjoy. I for one will be happy to turn my back on this..."

Mark was looking doubtful. "That may be a dangerous plan John. Supposing the shots were heard?" He pointed at the car Max had borrowed. "And what about that?"

John said: "Mark, we are half a mile from your nearest neighbors. Any problem and I will tell them that I was killing a few rabbits on the ridge. The car? No problem. It goes with me tonight and it disappears. And think of Helmut. If you involve the police then his part in this must come out into the open. He killed Max, and we helped in one way or another. Just see it my way. The matter is closed."

He pointed at Gustav. "Thanks to this man, the whole matter of the restoration of the money to the Bormanns has now been properly dealt with. Both sides of it. Yes — there is the unresolved matter of Paul Jacobs and the rest, but the cause of it all is here, and he is dead and finished. Why not leave it at that?"

"Helmut asked: "What do we do with him?"

John said: "Just leave it to me." He put a hand on Mark's shoulder. "Mark, I do not know entirely what Max Schwabl tried to put you through while we were elsewhere, but I imagine that it was something of a trial. As it happens, I think you have had enough. You and Sue have been following this tortuous trail of wickedness all summer, and halfway into the Autumn. It has dominated your lives I know, and all for no personal profit. If there is any justice left in the world, you are going to be at the end of some profound and well-deserved thanks before long. What I am asking you to do is leave the tidying up to me. We will put him in the garden shed for the moment. Let's get ready to greet the ladies. Not a word to anyone. Let's enjoy a marvelous celebration dinner. Where do you keep your beer Mark?

They all agreed. Mum's the word. They moved Max into the obscurity of the distant garden shed, and repaired to the kitchen. Out came the beer. Yes, there was some anxiety amongst them, but it was overlaid with relief. The forthcoming gaiety was going to easy to enjoy. This was not going to be a wake. It was a celebration.

Mark left them for a short time, going to use the 'phone in the library. He found Hal on his mobile. "Hal — the danger has gone. Don't ask me to explain. I may never be able to tell you how or why, but be reassured. You can take a relieved deep breath, and allow life to return to normal."

The mystified Hal could almost be heard taking the deep breath. He was silent for a moment. "Good. Thanks Mark." There was now mutual affection and trust between these two, and they agreed to keep in touch.

At one point over pre-dinner cocktails, Sue said to Mark: "I wish we knew where Schwabl was. It is just impossible to relax knowing that he may not be far away. He is sure to have us in his sights now. We must be the next target."

Mark took her hand. "I cannot tell you much for the moment, but I can assure you of one thing. He is no longer going to be a danger to us." He would not elaborate. Sue was consoled. She thought he meant that they had been informed of his arrest.

The Bormanns came by Mark and Sue's house the next morning to say goodbye. Gustav brought them in his car. He was going to take them back to London Airport, and pick up Olga who was on her way in the other direction. The Richters were to guest with Mark and Sue for a couple of days. The pressure was off. There were smiles all round.

Coffee cups in hand, Mark and Helmut stood by the French window, looking over the garden. Russet leaves were dropping from the oak tree at the bottom, stirred by the breeze. Mark gave Helmut an envelope, containing a check for the bribe money, and an explanatory note. They had not known about it. "Wait until you get home." said Mark. Then, almost as an afterthought he said: "Helmut. We came home last night and left you to it, glasses in hand, singing incomprehensible German folk songs with Mother's tinkling on the piano. Did John deal with the problem of Max's body?"

Helmut looked at Mark, a twinkle in his eye. "Mark. You have a secret to keep. Not only for the sake of the rest of us, but also for the sake of your wonderful mother."

Mark was puzzled. "Come on then Helmut. Reveal all."

"We had to get up at the crack of dawn to do it, but Max is now six feet down in Gunther's grave."

Printed in the United Kingdom
by Lightning Source UK Ltd.
105936UKS00001B/55